FREE BASEBALL

SUE CORBETT

SCHOLASTIC INC.
New York Toronto London Auckland Sydney
Mexico City New Delhi Hong Kong Buenos Aires

This book is a work of fiction. Names, characters, places, and incidents are either the product of the author's imagination or are used fictitiously, and any resemblance to actual persons, living or dead, business establishments, events, or locales is entirely coincidental.

ISBN-13: 978-0-545-07897-9
ISBN-10: 0-545-07897-0

Published by Scholastic Inc., 557 Broadway, New York, NY 10012, by arrangement with Dutton Children's Books, a division of Penguin Young Readers Group, a member of Penguin Group (USA) Inc.

12 11 10 9 8 7 6 5 4 3 2 1 8 9 10 11 12 13/0

Printed in the U.S.A. 40

First Scholastic printing, April 2008

Designed by Heather Wood

To the baseball men in my life,

Conor, Liam, and Tom

and to

Mike Veeck.

Without his Miracle,

the only baseball man in my life

would be Mookie.

free base·ball *n.* term for a game that gives fans more than they technically paid for–extra innings or the second game of a doubleheader.

The Lineup

The Crack of the Bat

The place on earth Felix Piloto loved best was a spot of red dirt two-thirds of the way toward third from second. Deep in the hole, his body folded nearly in half, his mitt dangling so close to the ground it blocked its own shadow.

Which is why it was so unusual that he was wishing he was somewhere else–so out of character for him to be caught off guard when a high chopper nearly clipped him in the chin. Felix was good at anticipating the odd bounce, but he'd been distracted–looking at the sun, instead of at the plate–trying to figure out what time it was and how soon he could ask to leave.

Plus, the Tigers were supposed to be practicing dead-fish bunts, ground balls that traveled just a few feet before rolling into no-man's-land out of any fielder's reach.

"JAKE! WHAT IN THE NAME OF THE BAMBINO WAS THAT?" Coach Drew threw his hands in the air.

Even after first bobbling the ball, Felix fired to the bag in plenty of time to throw out Jake.

Coach Drew showed the first baseman his open mitt, signaling him to throw the ball. "Jake! Have you ever seen a dead-fish fly?"

Jake scuffed the dirt in the base path, trudging back to the batter's box. "Dad, I *tried* to deaden it!"

"Let's go over this one more time, guys." Coach Drew took off his black cap with the big orange *T* and smoothed his hair. He always did this to calm himself down. The two boys who batted before Jake had failed to lay down decent bunts either. "What do you call a bunt hit into the air?"

"An out," a few of the guys mumbled.

"Flex your knees, square your shoulders, TAP the ball. Not SWING at the ball. TAP the ball." Coach Drew turned to face the infield. "Felix, what's that saying again?"

Ugh, why did I ever mention this? Felix asked himself. "*Dele un beso,*" he shouted, bracing himself for the taunting he knew was coming. Sure enough, he heard Carlos and the others squeak out kissy-face noises from the bench. He smiled and turned his backside toward them, showing where they could put their kisses. That set off the usual round of hoots, too.

"De-lay oon bay-so." Coach Drew turned the words around in his mouth, like he had a sunflower seed stuck in his teeth. "'Give it a kiss.' Felix, show them how to do it one more time, please."

Felix trotted in, flinging his mitt to Jake who tossed it to Carlos. He picked up the bat Jake had dropped and crouched into his stance. Coach Drew threw him a fastball. Felix turned toward the mound and loosened his grip, letting the bat slide a little in his palms. He aimed the bat so it met the ball head-on with a gentle smack, shooting it into the grass between the mound and the third-base line.

It dribbled to the edge of the turf and came to a complete stop.

"You guys see that?" Coach Drew had given this speech before. "*That* is a perfectly executed bunt! *That* gets you on base every blasted time."

Felix didn't bother running it out. Nobody had even tried to field the ball. Coach finally walked a few steps to his right and cupped the ball into his glove.

"Coach?" Felix was hoping he had earned a little "time off for good behavior," as Coach called it, because he wanted to get home as soon as possible.

"Your dad teach you how to do that, Felix?"

"No, his mother!" somebody on the bench shouted, and the kissing noises started up again.

Ha, Felix thought, like Mami would ever teach me anything about baseball. Will she even come to *any* of my games this year? "Okay if I go now? I've got a ton of homework."

"Get out of here, Felix. Time off for good behavior," he said, saving his growl for the other Tigers. "Carlos! Take Felix's spot at short. Jake! Get back in the batter's box and start kissing these baseballs!"

Felix stuffed his glove into his backpack and slung the heavy sack over his narrow shoulders. He had a brick at the bottom of the bag because he was trying to build up his shoulder and arm strength. He could bunt all right. But he wasn't much of a home-run threat.

• • •

Felix was only a little sorry about the white lie he told Coach about his homework. He never asked to leave baseball practice early, but he had a date with the radio.

For the past couple of weeks, Hot 102 had been giving away tickets to the season opener of the hometown team, the East Naples Egrets. The Egrets were a mediocre team in the Florida League. In baseball terms, playing for the Egrets was one step above playing for East Naples High School, but it was the first rung, the bottom rung, on the ladder that led to the Major Leagues.

The Egrets arrived in East Naples just the year before, when the town built them a new stadium at the edge of the swamp. The stadium had an official name that had something to do with a bank, but the newspaper had nicknamed it "The Bird's Nest," and that caught on. Felix was dying to see it, but his mother either had to work or had a class or was too tired or out of money. She always had an excuse.

Felix thought the real reason was that she just didn't like baseball anymore. She used to. Or so she said.

Getting a ticket to an Egrets game was not hard–free general admission tickets could be had for three proofs of purchase from HealthNut Wheat Bread. But Felix's mother bought Cuban bread from the *panadería*–white bread with a crunchy crust that Felix loved. And these other tickets were within his reach. He just had to win the call-in contest.

So every afternoon, he'd been racing home to turn on the radio, listening intently for the crack of the bat. That sound was the signal to call in. He had tried to win for two weeks already, putting the radio station's number on the speed dial. He kept the portable phone near his right hand, next to his math book. But no matter how quickly he grabbed the phone and hit *9, all he heard at the other end was a too-fast busy signal–*bzz bzz bzz*–the kind of noise you hear when the other phone is out of order.

Felix let himself into his empty house and turned on the radio before putting down his backpack. The aroma of the *frijoles negros* his mother had put in the Dutch oven before she went to work made his stomach rumble. He got a spoon from the drawer.

He was blowing steam off a spoonful of beans when he heard the crack of the bat. He put the spoon in his mouth, leaped for the phone, and pounded *9. He was puffing short breaths on the food–*huh! huh! huh!*–because it was way too hot to eat, when he was startled by the sound of the phone *ringing* at the other end of the line.

Felix swallowed the food quickly. It scorched his throat as it went down. He thought he might die. He hopped up and down to take his mind off the pain.

"HOT 102! YOU'RE OUR NINTH CALLER! YOU'RE GOING TO OPENING NIGHT AT THE BIRD'S NEST!"

Felix had run to get a gulp of water from the faucet, trying to cool off his mouth so he could speak.

"WHO'S OUR LUCKY WINNER?" The silence had gone on a beat longer than it should have.

Felix looked at the radio, as if he expected to see Len Randy, the announcer, there in the flesh. His reply would go out over the air. Radio waves would carry his voice across Florida and the Caribbean, perhaps as far as Cuba, where he was born. Would his *father* hear his voice?

"DO WE HAVE A LUCKY WINNER, OR IS THIS STATE-OF-THE-ART EQUIPMENT FAILING ME AGAIN? ENGINEERING? ANYBODY? HOW ABOUT CALLER NUMBER TEN? DO WE HAVE CALLER NUMBER TEN ON LINE TWO?"

"Yes! Yes! I'm caller nine!" Felix shouted.

"Great! You gonna tell us your name or should we try to guess? We could make a contest out of that, too–*guess* the name of the lucky winner. The prize'll be a date with our crack sound engineer." Len Randy snickered.

"Felix . . . Felix Piloto."

"Now we're getting places. Where ya calling from today, Felix?"

Felix had a moment of panic. His mother had repeatedly told him not to tell strangers where he lived. Did this count? He *had* to have those tickets.

"369SoutheastTwoHundredandThirtyNinthAvenueEastNaples Florida33327." He blurted it out fast, so no one could really understand what he was saying.

"Felix is suddenly FULL of information!" Len Randy said. "You a baseball fan, Felix?"

"Yes. My father *plays* baseball." He tensed. If his father *was* listening, now he would know the Felix Piloto on the radio was the same Felix Piloto who was his son. He should have mentioned his father's name–Claudio de la Portilla, a member of the

Cuban National Team, a left fielder so good people called his glove *"Dónde se triplica va a morir"*–where triples go to die.

"Take Pop to the game and tell him it's on Hot 102. Now, tell me, Felix, what radio station has South Central Florida's GREATEST GIVEAWAYS?"

"Hot 102?" Felix realized too late he should have tried to sound more excited, but the suggestion he take his father to the game jolted him. I wish, he thought.

Len Randy must have been disgusted with him–he put Felix on hold and gave the weather report.

Felix felt the roof of his mouth with his tongue, wondering if he had done permanent damage. Possibly.

But getting the tickets was worth it.

When he heard Mami's car clank into the driveway, Felix ran to the front door. He spilled the details in an excited rush while she dropped her bag onto a table and took off her coat.

"You are calling strangers on the telephone while I am at work?"

"They're not strangers. It's a radio station."

"But what if I needed to reach you to know you are fine?"

He noticed she didn't say she had *tried* to call, which he was sure she hadn't. His mother was on a mission to get a better job, so they could buy a house or, at least, live somewhere nicer than the duplex they rented now, from a landlord who appeared only when the rent was due. "You're missing the point, Mami. How else was I supposed to get to see a real baseball game?"

"Baseball, baseball. There is more to life than baseball, Felix."

"Not mine, there isn't."

"And what is that supposed to mean?"

"Nothing." Why had he thought she might be happy he won the tickets?

"How was school? That is a part of life that interests me," she called from the kitchen. He turned and saw her lift the lid on the beans, swirling a wooden spoon through them.

"Boring."

She looked about to respond to that when the phone rang. "*Hola*," she said, before pausing. "*Ay, Fabi. ¿Cómo estás?*"

Her friend, Fabiola. Dinner would be a while. Felix went to his room to get his mitt. There was still enough daylight to toss the ball around.

He grabbed his glove from his dresser, where it sat next to a framed photograph of his father–the only photograph Felix had of him. Tía Lupe gave it to him, wrapped in tissue paper, when Felix and Mami left their house in Hialeah to move to East Naples. Felix hadn't wanted to move. Even though he hadn't started school then, he had friends in the neighborhood, and Tía Lupe and Tío Toni's house always had people coming and going who made a fuss over him, bringing him candy, taking his picture.

"That was part of my reason *for* moving away–the constant people," his mother told him a year or two later, after Felix wondered why they lived on their own, rather than with his father's relatives. "You needed to be left alone," she'd said, but when Felix tried to get her to explain what that meant, she waved him off.

Felix tilted the photograph in his hand now, trying to figure out if he looked like his father, who he couldn't remember. His father wore a red jersey, with *Cuba* written in white script across his chest. He had a bat over his shoulder and a look of concentration on his face, as if he were really waiting for a pitch.

"You would be excited about free tickets to the Egrets game, right, Papi?" Felix asked the photo, remembering the deejay's suggestion that he "take Pop to the game." He set the photo down, next to the scuffed baseball he also kept on his dresser.

"Felix Piloto de la Portilla! *¡Venga aquí en este momento!*"

What did I do now? Felix wondered.

Mami had her hand cupped over the telephone receiver. "Fabi heard you on the radio!"

"So?"

"She says you gave out your address!"

"They asked for it!"

"*Dios mio*, Felix! Are you trying to give the kidnappers a map?"

"I didn't say I was alone."

"*Ay*, Felix. No good. How are you even going to get to this game?"

"There are two tickets."

She took her hand from the receiver. "He wants me to take him."

"Can't you take one night off?"

His mother gave him a long look while she listened to Fabi. The circles under her dark eyes looked deeper than usual. "Hang on," she said into the phone. "Fabi says this game is on April 5."

Felix nodded. "Next Thursday."

"A *school* night?"

"Mami, *por favor.*" Felix put his hands together to plead. "It's opening night. The game starts at seven. It'll be over by bedtime." Or what would be my bedtime if I lived with a normal mother and not one who treats me like I'm still a baby, Felix thought.

"On a school night, no less," she said into the receiver. "Felix, no more radio contests. *¿Entiendes, m'ijo?"*

"Sí, Mami, I understand," Felix said, but he didn't.

Mami picked up her conversation with Fabi, while Felix headed outside. He let the front door slap shut behind him. He sat on the step and put his mitt down at his feet. He didn't feel like tossing the ball anymore. He couldn't figure it out. He knew his mother wanted a better job and a nicer place to live. He knew that meant going to night school and working overtime, which meant missing a lot of his games.

But how–*how in the name of the Bambino*–could anyone think winning free tickets to a real baseball game was a bad thing?

Jersey Night

2 The school day on April 5 seemed to stretch to twice its normal length. Math class dragged on exponentially. For the first time ever, even recess seemed longer than it actually was. The afternoon announcements went on and on and on while Felix, first in line at the door of his portable classroom, was coiled like a spring, waiting.

When the principal finally said, "Fifth- and sixth-grade walkers and car riders are dismissed," Felix took the wooden steps in a single leap, intending to run the whole way home, with the brick at the bottom of his book bag banging against his back.

"Hey, Felix! Wait up."

Felix reluctantly hit the brakes when he heard Jake calling him.

"You want to come to the batting cage with my dad and me?" Jake asked.

Normally, Felix would have tried to borrow Coach Drew's cell phone to see if it was okay with Mami. "I can't today."

"What's up?"

"I have tickets to the Egrets' opener tonight."

"Cool," Jake said. "I went to a few games last year. Did you try the pitching machine? What was your speed?"

"I haven't been to a game yet."

"Y'know, the game doesn't start till after dinner. We can get you back in time."

"I have to have my homework done before or . . ." Felix's voice trailed off.

"Or your mom won't let you go."

"Right."

"Okay—well, see you at practice tomorrow." They had reached the sidewalk and Jake broke left toward the parent pickup line. Felix could see Coach Drew leaning against the hood of his truck, talking with somebody's mother. He felt a stab of jealousy. No one was ever waiting to pick him up from school. His father never took him to the batting cage or to ball games where he could have the speed of his throw clocked by a radar gun.

But he fought down those feelings. Tonight he *was* going. Maybe Mami would even enjoy it, and she would start coming to the Tigers' games. After all, Felix thought, he wouldn't even exist if his mother hadn't been a baseball fan once—that was how she met his father.

Felix kicked a rock from the sidewalk, thinking of all the times he asked Mami to tell him about how she caught a foul ball hit into the stands by the All-Star outfielder, Claudio de la Portilla.

She'd begin by correcting him. "Actually, Felito, I didn't catch it. It rolled to my feet and I picked it up. In Cuba it's not like here, though. The fans have to return the balls because there aren't enough to spare."

Felix remembered being small enough to sit on her lap for this story. "So if you gave it back, how come I have it?" he'd ask, already knowing the answer.

"When your father came to the railing, he said, 'Can you bring it to me after the game?' and he winked."

"Because you're so pretty," Felix would tell her.

She'd kiss his forehead and continue. "Then after the game, when I tried again to return it, he said, 'You can keep the souvenir if you will let me take you to dinner.'"

"And here's the ball," Felix would say, holding it up. "Your souvenir."

"The ball and you." Often Mami would have tears in her eyes by this part of the story.

Felix could picture the ball now as he fit his key into the front door lock. He kept the ball on the worn wooden top of his dresser, a piece of furniture he and Mami took from somebody's curb in a neighborhood with sidewalks and wide green lawns. Now the ball leaned against the photograph of his father, but Felix remembered a time when he would sleep with it. He'd grown out of that, of course, but this ball had probably been *touched* by his father—caught in his glove and rifled back to the infield with his bare hand—before his bat sent it spinning into the crowd.

Felix shrugged off his backpack and noticed the light on the answering machine, flashing slowly. He tucked his house key, which he wore on a long braided rope, back inside his shirt, where it often tangled with his St. Christopher medal. He pushed the button beneath the blinking light.

"*M'ijo.*" Mami's voice. "We are having a crisis here. I hate to do this, but . . ."

Felix stamped his foot. No! Not again! He put his fingers in his ears. If I don't listen, this can't happen.

"I know what you are thinking, Felix, but you are wrong."

Felix took his fingers out of his ears.

"I have not forgotten the big game. I got Maryann to go with you. I'll pick you up at six. Do your homework now. *Lo siento, m'ijo. Te amo.*"

Maryann Lester? This could not be happening. Felix played the message again. Go to the game with a babysitter? With a *lousy* babysitter–someone who watched soap operas on TV the entire time she was supposed to be working?

He hit the speed dial on the phone.

"Connie Piloto. May I help you?"

"Mami, I can't go to the game with that stupid girl!"

"Felix, be reasonable. I can run out of here and get you and Maryann to the stadium, or you can stay home."

"But she's a jerk! And I am too old for a babysitter!" When Felix turned ten he had convinced his mother that the money she paid Maryann to watch TV was better stashed in the pouch where they kept their "new house" fund.

"I know that, Felito, but this is unavoidable."

"Just like it was unavoidable that you made it to only one of my games last year?"

"Felix, that has nothing to do with this. We were installing a new mainframe last spring. There was an emergency almost every night." She let out a breath in a huff. "I know you will find this hard to believe, Felix, but I don't actually *like* working all this overtime. That is why I am going to college. When I get my degree, I will get a better-paying job, and then I will take you to baseball games."

Felix sighed. He'd heard this before.

"What if I got Jake to go with me?"

"Two eleven-year-olds alone at a baseball game?"

"We won't be alone. The game is a sellout. Plus, Jake is twelve."

"*Ay*, Felix, call and ask his mother if he can go. Don't ask Jake. Ask his *mother*."

Felix called Jake, but got the answering machine. He called Carlos, who couldn't go–it was his brother's birthday.

Pedro. Grounded for a D in math on his last report card.

Finally, he got Nick.

"Wow! Free tickets? You bet, I'll go," Nick said. "Hang on, let me ask my mom," he said, putting down the phone.

Felix took a deep breath of relief. Going to a baseball game with Maryann Lester would be worse than not going at all.

"Felix? Sorry, man. She said, 'No way.'"

"No way?"

"She said I could go if your parents were going but not just by ourselves. She's a major-league worrywart."

"She has a twin."

"Who?"

"My mother."

At six o'clock, Felix glared out of the passenger window at Maryann Lester, who was sitting on her front stoop, a purple balloon of gum inflating and exploding on her lips, while she filed her nails. She had a copy of *Teen People* on her lap and a bottle of nail polish balanced on her knee.

"Hey, Mrs. Piloto," she said, plopping into the backseat.

"Hello, Maryann." Felix's mom waited for Maryann to buckle her seat belt before putting the car in gear. "How are you enjoying high school?"

"Every bit as bad as middle school," Maryann said.

"*Qué lastima*. Maybe it will pick up." Felix's mom glanced in the rearview mirror. "I wouldn't do that here," she warned. Maryann had her fingers splayed on the magazine and the open bottle of polish gripped between her knees. "The shocks in this car are gone."

"Plus, we might suffocate." Felix cranked down his window.

Maryann tightened the cap on the nail polish. "I'll do it at the game then. Baseball is s-o-o-o boring."

Not that I would care if *Maryann* suffocated, he thought.

A line of cars snaked out of The Bird's Nest, so Felix's mother dropped them at the edge of the stadium's parking lot.

"I'll keep the radio tuned to the game so I will know when it's over," she said. "I'll pick you up right here. Have fun!"

Fun. Like that was possible. Felix slammed the door and headed for the turnstiles, where he had to wait until Maryann sauntered up.

"If we hurry we might see the end of batting practice," he said.

"Oh, whoop-de-do."

It made him almost physically ill to hand his second ticket

to a person who thought a baseball game was a good chance to polish her nails. But at least he was here, he thought, trying to shake off his anger. He would ignore her.

"It's Jersey Night," the usher said, passing Felix a limp blue shirt. Cool, thought Felix. He put it on. The Egrets were not his favorite team, but a free shirt is a free shirt.

Felix had his seat number memorized–he had looked at the tickets ten times a day since they came in the mail: Box A, row three, seats one and two. As he entered the stadium, his eyes fell first on the bright field–grass so green it looked fake, like the plastic stuff in the Easter basket Mami gave him. Signs in primary colors lined the outfield fence–advertisements for Spratley Insurance and Red Hot Franks. The scoreboard, with its electric lights, towered over center field.

Wow, Felix thought, imagine playing *here*. His field didn't have any lights. All the games had to be played before the sun set.

He scanned the signs and found Box A. "Wow! We're right behind home plate!"

"Dexter!" Maryann called out to someone. She headed in the direction she was waving–toward left field.

"Maryann, our seats are down here." Felix pointed in the other direction.

"Let's go sit with my friends."

"But these are the best seats in the stadium. *Box seats*."

Maryann pushed out her hip and rested her clenched fist on it. "Felix, I'm in charge and I say where we're sitting. I've got my cell phone. Should we call your mother?"

"We don't have tickets to sit with your friends. Those are somebody else's seats. The game is sold out."

"Fine. We can just sit with them until the ushers toss us. See? A compromise."

Felix felt his dislike of Maryann Lester bubble in his gut.

Maryann's friends–two teenage goons with spiked hair named Dexter and Scotty–had seats in the bleachers. No one ever did come around to check their tickets.

"Peewee–go get us peanuts," Dexter said, tickling the side of Felix's face with a ten-dollar bill.

"Get them yourself." Felix had bought a program with the money he had. He wanted to keep score.

"Friendly booger," Dexter said to Maryann.

"Don't pay any attention to him. I don't," she said. "Want me to get the stuff?"

"No, I'll go." Dexter hit Felix sharply with his knees as he got up.

"Cut it out, jerk," Felix barked.

"Ooh, Peewee has a temper."

Felix stared straight ahead and forced himself to calm down. I will not let these morons ruin the game.

People continued to stream in while Felix wrote the player names on his scorecard. The Egrets' opponent was a team from West Lauderdale called The Miracle. He wondered which Major

League club The Miracle was affiliated with. Felix read every inch of baseball news the paper ran, so he knew some farm teams had the same name as the parent club, and some had related names–the Egrets, for instance, fed players to the Baltimore Orioles. Felix kept track of these things because he knew if his father could get to Florida, he would start in the minor leagues, like the great Yankees pitcher El Duque did, after he escaped from Cuba. Felix spent a lot of time staring out the window of his portable classroom at Sawgrass Shores Elementary, wondering which Major League team would sign his father, and where the three of them would wind up living.

But he couldn't think of a Major League team that had anything to do with miracles. Maybe the California Angels? He didn't know much about the Angels because they never came to Florida to play, but he had seen a movie about them when he slept over at Jake's once. He remembered it was really sad.

Felix recognized the names of some of the Egrets players from last year's team, which he knew was bad news for those players. It meant they hadn't gotten any closer to being promoted to the big club. And there were two players on The Miracle whose names stopped him–Santiago Diaz, the catcher, who batted fifth, and an outfielder named Bobby *Piloto*! Felix wondered if either of them was actually from Cuba or if they just had Cuban names. If they grew up in Cuba, would they know his father? If Felix had gotten here earlier, he could have gone down to the railing and tried to get their attention. Maybe I can do that after the game, he thought.

Ha. Like Maryann will let me. Tough luck, he decided. He would do it anyway.

Dexter came back carrying a cardboard tray, just as the public-address announcer asked fans to rise for the national anthem. A girl came out to a microphone near home plate and sang. If I was sitting in my real seat, Felix thought, I would actually hear the umpire yell, "Play ball!" He wondered if he should just get up and go sit in the seat he had won. Would Maryann really call his mother? His mother didn't like to get phone calls at work. "Not unless it is '*una emergencia,*'" she always said.

This wouldn't qualify as an emergency, Felix knew.

He sat down and regretted it. He had sat in something wet. He stood. There was a pool of dark liquid on the bench. He was confused until Dexter asked, "Want a sip of my Coke, Peewee?"

Felix fought an urge to knock the soda out of Dexter's hands. I will just go to my own seat. She can find me after the game. He gathered up his stuff and was making his way out of the row when Maryann called, "Five-nine-five . . ." She had her cell phone in her hand and was pressing the buttons.

Instead, Felix walked up the bleachers and sat in an empty seat in the row behind them. Dexter called out, loud enough for everyone around to hear, "Have an accident, Peewee?"

Felix felt his face turn red. The game, he told himself. Think about the game.

"Don't cry, Peewee," Dexter said. "Here's a tissue." Dexter held out a napkin, then dropped it when Felix reached for it.

Scotty and Dexter laughed. "Oh, leave him alone," Maryann said, "or he'll tell his mommy."

For the rest of the night they tortured him. Dexter threw his peanut shells in an arc over his head. Scotty would watch and yell, "Bull's-eye!" if one hit Felix. Very few did because Felix dodged them. But he spent more time avoiding peanut shells than he did watching the game, which was a pitchers' duel until the seventh. He gave up trying to keep track of the pitch count. He was determined not to leave his seat until the game was over, sure if he did, he'd be pelted with peanuts or worse on the way down the steps.

Felix fumed. Why are these idiots here? They didn't watch a bit of the game. He couldn't wait to tell his mother how her babysitting idea worked out.

In the top of the seventh, the Egrets' pitcher got into trouble. He gave up a single to the first batter, walked the second, and loaded the bases by hitting the third with a curveball that curved the wrong way.

The game paused while the reliever warmed up, then The Miracle's catcher, Santiago Diaz, strode to the plate. The Egrets were the home team, but Felix found himself silently pulling for Diaz, a husky player with the same color skin Felix had, a color his mother called *café con leche*—coffee with milk. Diaz took two pitches, both way inside, before smashing a high fastball out of the park.

"A grand slam!" Felix shouted, unable to catch himself. The people around him glared.

"Don't you know which team's which, Peewee?" Dexter asked.

Felix kept his eyes on Diaz as he circled the bases. His teammates waited for him at home plate and thumped his broad shoulders when he crossed it. What a great feeling that must be, Felix thought.

The inning ended quietly after that, with The Miracle ahead, 4-0. During the seventh-inning stretch, the public-address announcer reminded everyone about the "Diamond Dash." Felix had seen a sign for it, but until the announcer explained it, he hadn't known what it was. Kids under twelve were allowed to run the bases after the game! Felix couldn't believe it. He definitely wanted to do that.

"Oh, no you're not, runt," Maryann said when the game ended and Felix said he was going to get on the Diamond Dash line. "Your mother said she'd meet us outside right after the game ended."

"Try to stop me." Felix walked off toward the end of the long line.

"Let Peewee go," Dexter said, tugging Maryann by the belt loop of her jeans. "C'mon, walk me to the gate."

"I'll meet you right here!" she called. Felix didn't even turn around. He got in line behind a younger boy, who was holding a woman's hand. The woman brought the boy's hand to her face and kissed the back of it. Felix looked away.

He had a mountain of anger inside him–anger at Dexter for picking on him and at Maryann for letting him, but especially at Mami, for not getting *one lousy night* off from work. Tears came to his eyes, so he stared into the scoreboard, trying to focus on something else–the runs, the hits, the errors, tomorrow's likely starting pitcher–until he realized someone was calling him. The line had moved and he hadn't.

"You okay, buddy?" It was the usher.

"Yeah," Felix said, wiping his eyes. "Allergies."

"Okay–you're next. Let 'er rip."

Felix trotted to home plate. Wow. The stadium lights made him feel like he was in a movie. The field sparkled. He paused, taking it all in. He looked out over the center-field fence, where Diaz's grand-slam ball had sailed. He remembered the sound of the bat thudding against the leather ball. He started running. He ran fast, like he was trying to stretch a long single into a double. He dug in his feet. Dirt flew as he rounded first base. He wished he was wearing his cleats so he could really sink into the clay of the infield, but . . . *he was going to make it to second without a throw anyway!*

The crowd cheered him on.

They were chanting his name!

Fel-ix! Fel-ix! Fel-ix!

The ball got away from the second baseman!

Felix hit the second-base bag and turned for third, never slowing. He looked up, searching the third-base coach's box for the sign. Should he hit the brakes? Did he need to slide? Or would he get the green light–try for a play at the plate . . .

But there was no coach in the third-base box. There was a smiling man with a camera, videotaping the boy in front of Felix, who had just rounded third.

"Slide into home, Danny!" the man shouted.

Danny's father. Felix slowed up. He didn't want to be in this other family's movie. He looked to his right, away from the smiling father. The tears he had blinked back flooded into his eyes again. He looked up–and saw Maryann at the railing, searching the field.

He looked away quickly. His eye caught the visitors' dugout, along the third-base line.

Felix had never been in a real dugout. When he reached third, he slid into the base, sending up a plume of rust-colored dust. He stood and brushed himself off. Then, instead of turning for home, he trotted to the dugout.

From the top step he saw Maryann, who was shading her eyes and scanning the field. Felix looked at the same scene–maybe a hundred boys and girls, some very small, some exactly Felix's size–any number of whom could be Felix. It'd be difficult to pick him out of the crowd. All the kids were wearing the same shirts–sky blue baseball jerseys with the word *Egrets* scripted across the front.

He turned and trotted down the next two steps, into the dugout, and then strode purposefully into the hallway that led to the locker room. He didn't look back to see if anyone was calling him. He just pretended he belonged there. He stopped once, in the dark tunnel, and mopped the wetness from his eyes with the tail of his new jersey.

The New Batboy

3 The locker room reverberated with noise—faucets running, toilets flushing, players laughing and giving each other high fives, low fives, and behind-the-back fives. A player walked by in nothing but a jockstrap and Felix, embarrassed, looked away.

"You hear that guy in the box behind their dugout? He had some great lines," a player called to no one in particular. "'Hey, ump! How can you sleep with all these lights on?'"

"We gotta tell that one to the Blue Review," another player said.

"We should take that guy with us," a third player said.

"Yeah, kidnap him—we need all the help we can get. You hear what he said when their pitcher walked you in the seventh? 'Now I know why there's only one *I* in umpire.'"

"That was an early birthday gift," the player said. "But with the way our luck crashed last year, I'll take it."

Felix wished he could dissolve into the wall, so he could keep listening to the conversation. He hadn't been able to make out what the fan they were talking about was yelling–only that he was getting a lot of laughs from the people around him. The guys on the Tigers would crack up over that line about the one-eyed umpire.

But there was nowhere to hide. Just as he began to feel self-conscious, Felix was caught. An older guy in baseball pants and an undershirt walked by, noticed him, and clutched him by the shoulder.

"You the boy they sent over? All the equipment bags need to go out." He gestured to a stack of canvas sacks by the door.

Felix wanted to ask "out where?" but the guy didn't let him get a word in.

"And make sure you get everybody's uni. I started a bag for laundry, but you'll need another one." The man nodded at a cotton hamper suspended on a wire stand, just as a player shot his crumpled-up jersey into the bag.

"He shoots, he scores!" the player said, flashing a grin at Felix and the old guy. "Great game, right, Cookie?"

Oh, this guy is the manager, Felix realized. He looked different without his hat and shirt. Cookie grinned at the player but didn't let go of Felix's shoulder.

"Make sure the laundry gets on the bus, too, or that's what they'll be wearing tomorrow night." He pointed at the player, who had stripped down to his underwear. "And I got enough problems with attendance as it is."

"Maybe that would *help* attendance, Cookie," a player shouted.

"Oh, nuts. Forget I mentioned it. That's about the only thing Mench hasn't tried. Naked baseball. Don't give him any ideas."

Laughter rippled around the room. Cookie unclenched Felix's shoulder and walked away while Felix wondered if he was talking about Vic Mench. Vic Mench was related to Will Mench, the Hall of Famer, and had something to do with baseball, too, but Felix couldn't remember what. He'd seen his name in the paper.

Some players were still half-dressed, waiting for their turn in the showers, so Felix took the equipment bags out first. He loved being mistaken for the batboy, enjoying not only being in the locker room and around a team, but also the idea of making Maryann sweat over not knowing where he was.

Of course, his mother was waiting, too. He felt guilty–but only for a second. He grunted as he hoisted the first equipment bag onto his shoulder. Serves Mami right, Felix thought, pushing open the door with his hip. If she would've just taken the night off, he wouldn't be in this situation. And she could hardly be mad at him after he told her how Maryann and her jerky friends ruined the game.

The night air was warm. Under the parking-lot lights, Felix saw a big silver bus a few hundred feet away. As he got closer, he could see a man leaning against the front of it, talking on a cell phone.

"Hang on," the man said into the phone. He called to Felix. "That the team's stuff?"

"Some of it. There's more inside," Felix told him.

"We got plenty of room." The man walked to the side of the bus and flipped up two silver hatches. "Stash it all in there–you can use both bins."

Felix wedged the bag in sideways and pushed it back as far as it would go–almost the width of the bus. He walked between the locker room and the bus with several more loads. Across the parking lot, he could see a train of red taillights. He wondered where his mother was in all that traffic. Was she even there yet? He thought about Maryann stewing, wondering where *he* was. Felix hoped she would get in trouble. Big trouble. Too bad he couldn't make it look like *he'd* been kidnapped, just to get Maryann in *more* trouble.

In the locker room the floor around the canvas hamper was littered with shots that had not scored. Felix picked the clothing up and stuffed everything into the bag, which was getting full. He slid the bag off its frame. Felix often did his and Mami's laundry at the Soap 'n' Suds. He carried their laundry on his back in a bag like this one, though their stuff never amounted to much. He was about to pull the string to close the neck when a voice called out.

"*¡Un momento, niño!*"

Felix lifted his head. Diaz, the catcher, walked toward him with his game clothes in his big hands. "*Uno mas,*" he said–one more–and then he looked down at his feet and shook his head.

Felix thought he knew what had happened, because it still happened occasionally to Mami. She would say something in Spanish without meaning to because, as she said, the words came into her brain that way before the English words did.

"*Gracias, señor,*" Felix said quickly, to let him know he understood.

A smile broke across Diaz's face. *"Ay! Tú hablas español."*

Felix nodded. "Great hit!" he said and, again, he noted the confusion in Diaz's eyes. Felix laughed. The English words had come into his head first. *"¡Su cuadrangular era magnífico!"* Felix took a big pretend swing for emphasis.

"¡Ay! El 'homer,'" Diaz said. *"Sí, era muy bueno. Gracias."* He turned to go but stopped and asked, *"¿Es el chico de equipo?"*

Felix didn't want to lie and say he *was* the batboy, although it dawned on him he would really *like* to be the batboy. So he gave the smallest nod and left it at that, stuffing Diaz's dirty uniform into the bag.

"No tienes la camisa correcto, m'ijo," Diaz said, and he pointed at Felix's jersey. Felix looked at his shirt. The *wrong* shirt, Diaz had called it. True. Why would The Miracle's batboy be wearing an Egrets jersey?

Cookie came by in his street clothes and clapped Diaz on the back. "Shower up, star of the game. The bus leaves in ten minutes." He kept walking.

Diaz looked at Felix. Without saying a word, Felix knew Diaz needed a translation, so Felix told him what Cookie had said.

"Ay! Gracias," Diaz said, jogging off to the showers. He called back, *"Hasta luego?"*

"Sí–hasta luego," Felix said. Another lie. He wouldn't see him again later. Felix wished he had stalled Diaz a little longer–to ask if he was from Cuba, or if he knew his father. What a dummy I am, he thought. He shouldered the laundry bag and used it to bang open the door to the parking lot. Maybe he could come to the game the next time The Miracle played the

Egrets. But would Diaz remember him and realize he lied about being the batboy?

How could I really get a job like this? Felix wondered. This is where I belong–with a real baseball team. The feeling he got from being in The Miracle's locker room was nothing like being in the dugout with the Tigers. Half the kids on his team were only there because their parents wanted them to be, or because they had nothing better to do. He wondered if the Egrets already had a boy who did this. But he knew what his mother would say. He had offered before to get a job to help save money. Mami always told him no, working could wait.

"*M'ijo*, you have your whole life for a job but only one chance at an education. First things first," she'd said. Meanwhile, they had to scavenge furniture from the stuff other people threw away.

Felix was so busy thinking–about the missed chance with Diaz, about how he might talk Mami into letting him apply for a batboy's job–that he almost missed the announcement entirely. But it registered somewhere in his brain that he had heard his name, and so he stopped to listen. Straining, he heard the voice of the public-address announcer inside the stadium.

"Felix Piloto. Report immediately to Gate A.
Your babysitter *is waiting for you."*

The way the announcer said *babysitter*, Felix could tell he was laughing about it.

Felix wasn't laughing. Even in the dark, he felt his face redden. *His babysitter?* Did she have to say that? He had a thought that made him almost nauseous–what if the guys in the locker room knew he had come to the game with a *babysitter*? He would die of shame. He shifted the laundry on his shoulder, wishing he could stuff himself inside the bag, take himself away from rotten Maryann Lester, and even from his mother, who didn't care enough about him to take a night off when he had worked so hard to get the tickets. The anger he had swallowed earlier came roaring back. He hated them both! Tears swelled into his eyes. He blinked hard, fighting them down.

The bus driver was still talking on his cell phone. Felix slotted the last bag into the hold. He shut the hatch on one bin. He looked around. The driver was gesturing with his hand, deep in some story. The parking lot was empty but for Felix and the chatty driver.

He crouched before the second bin to look at the hatch. Was there a way to open it from the inside? Maybe. He depressed a lever that seemed to release the locking mechanism.

He looked around again.

Then he climbed into the bin. Just to see if he would fit, he told himself.

He slotted his lean frame between an equipment bag and the dirty laundry. He reached out his long arm and brought the hatch toward him. He pulled it shut and lay very still. It was so dark he couldn't see anything but paper-thin seams of light where the edges of the hatch met the body of the bus. He groped for the lever, found it, and pushed it down.

It opened.

Here was his chance to get out. Find his mother. Go home.

Home. Where tomorrow afternoon he would do his homework alone, until Mami called and said, "Go ahead and eat, Felito. I am going to be late again. *Lo siento.*"

I'm not going back to that, Felix decided. She probably won't even miss me. She won't have to come home from work at all. She can stay there all night.

He pulled the hatch shut again, then dried his eyes with the back of his hand. The laundry was warm and smelly, but it was more comfortable to squeeze up against that than against the equipment bag. The metal floor felt cold. Felix took a deep breath to calm himself, to *reassure* himself that there would be air to breathe.

A few minutes later, the engine roared to life. The bus traveled just a short distance–probably to the clubhouse door, Felix figured, because the next sensation he felt was the steady bouncing of heavy footsteps–men getting on the bus and walking to their seats above his head. He listened intently but could hear nothing clearly.

Then the bus shifted into gear again. Felix curled against the laundry bag as they bounced over rutted roads on the way to West Lauderdale, a place he had never been.

In the Hold

4 It took only minutes for Felix to decide that the baggage compartment of a bus—even a fairly nice bus like the one in which The Miracle rode home—is a horrible way to travel. He was more than hot and uncomfortable. He felt sure he had lived his last day on earth.

Every time the bus hit a pothole or a crack in the pavement, some part of his anatomy banged against the cold metal floor. What the baggage space gave in width, it took away in headroom. Lying on his side, Felix had about a foot and a half of air between his ear and the ceiling. He tried to wiggle the bags around so he could lie on his back, and maybe put his hands behind his head to cushion the bounces, but there was no room to maneuver. He worried the players above him would hear things shifting around unnaturally below. He settled for resting the side of his face against the dirty laundry bag, which meant holding his head at an odd angle. His neck started aching within minutes.

Beyond death, he had a second fear.

What if he lived?

What would happen when the bus parked? How soon would the luggage bins be opened and the stowaway detected? What lie could he tell to explain why he was in the luggage compartment? Could he say he had suddenly felt tired so he crawled inside the bin to nap, never meaning to be there when the bus pulled out? Would anybody believe that?

I wouldn't, Felix thought.

But as the trip went on—a half hour? an hour? ninety minutes?—Felix decided he didn't care what anybody believed. He just wanted out. He would live the rest of his days with the odor of diesel fumes in his nose, he thought. Or maybe that's how I'll die—poisoning rather than blunt trauma. He would do anything to see the hatch open now. He would be in trouble, punished by Mami, but . . .

Mami. Would she realize he had run away, or would she think he had been kidnapped? She was always warning him not to talk to strangers, not to get into the cars of people he didn't know. Would she think that was what had happened?

No, Felix decided. Mami was a runaway herself. She came to Florida smuggled inside a boat. Felix, not yet a year old, had clung to her neck. Not that he remembered that. She told him about it many times—how there were thirteen people in the dark, hot hold of the boat. No place to pee and someone threw up before the boat even made it out of Cuba's territorial waters.

Felix always sat on her lap for this story—where he imagined he'd also sat during the voyage across the Straits of Florida. She would stroke his hair and speak quietly. "Your father paid our way," Mami told him. "They didn't want to take me. Well, they didn't want to take *you*, because they didn't want a baby, but your father insisted. He wouldn't give them the money until they agreed. It was *you* he wanted out of there. We are here because he wanted something else for *you*."

Felix wondered what his father would think if his son died in the luggage compartment of a bus. *Estúpido!* That's what he would think. Felix made a vow: If he reached West Lauderdale alive, he would find a telephone and call Mami right away, to tell her he was okay.

Then he remembered he probably didn't have enough money to make a long-distance phone call. Could he call collect? He had seen the commercials on TV: 1-555-NO-COINS.

Just as his plan took shape, the bus slowed. Felix heard the air squish out of the brakes in a long hiss. He felt the bus make a wide turn and stop.

He was alive.

He was dead. What could he say? His pulse pinged even faster. His new Egrets jersey was soaked with sweat.

The bus rocked with the *thump-thump-thump* of heavy men bouncing down its steps. Felix heard voices, men calling good night to one another. "Batting practice at four!" someone shouted. He thought he recognized Cookie's voice. A car engine started in the distance, then another, then a third. No one opened the luggage compartment to get the team's stuff, so no one discovered him. Relieved, he realized the equipment and laundry must get taken care of in the morning.

Finally, the night quieted. He'd take a chance that the area around the bus was clear.

He depressed the lever on the inside of the hatch. It opened with a click so loud Felix was sure it would draw attention. He lay perfectly still, clean air streaming in through the wider opening. He took several deep breaths, then pushed the hatch a few inches more. He still couldn't see anything besides pavement, so he nudged it a few inches. It sprang up! Felix flinched. His heart hammered at the wall of his chest.

No one approached.

It took a few seconds for Felix's eyes to adjust as he shifted his gaze around the landscape that he could see from the baggage compartment. He saw a stadium and light spilling onto a concrete courtyard from an open office door. Then he saw a pair of legs in white athletic socks hiked up to the knees–the legs of an older man. The legs were coming toward the bus! Felix looked away, preparing for the moment he was caught. He squeezed his eyes shut. His body tensed.

"Dickey!" a voice called. "Mench is looking for you!"

"Aw, cripes," a second voice said. "What is it now?"

Felix looked up and saw the white-socked legs stop, turn, and walk back toward the stadium.

He inched his body out so he could see to the left. Blue pant legs–the bus driver–came down the steps and rested against the side of the bus.

Go away! Felix thought, pulling his body back an inch into the bin. Just then the tiny tinny ring of a cell phone floated on the air.

"Hello," the driver said. Felix heard footsteps clip-clopping away from the bus. He leaned out a little more and saw the driver heading toward the ballpark, his phone pressed to his ear.

This is my chance, Felix thought. He quickly pushed out the bags on either side of him. With the two bags out, he had enough room to turn around. He put his sneakered feet on the ground, and made the sign of the cross. Then, very slowly, he slid his body out of the luggage compartment and held himself in a deep crouch, like a catcher behind the plate. His head was spinning. He felt bruised and dizzy. He worried he might faint if he moved too fast, so he half stood first, his hands on his knees, his head below his waist. He knew that he shouldn't stand by the bus, in plain sight of whoever hadn't left the stadium yet, but he felt too sick to move. Finally, then slowly, he picked up his head. He was woozy, but he was okay.

He took a deep, grateful breath.

"M'ijo!" A hand touched his shoulder.

Felix jumped in fright. His head snapped around to see who had sneaked up behind him.

It was Diaz. *"¿Necesitas ayuda?"*

Felix tried hard not to react. He nodded, then eked out, *"Sí."* He could definitely use some help, and he was grateful it was Diaz, not the manager.

Diaz shouldered an equipment bag. *"No lo vi en el autobús."*

Felix reached into the bin to grab a bag so he wouldn't have to look at Diaz while he lied. "I took a nap," he told him, hoping that would explain why Diaz hadn't seen him on the bus. Then he remembered he needed to say it in Spanish. *"Tomé una siesta."*

"Ay," Diaz said, nodding. He picked up a second bag and headed toward the stadium.

Felix walked a half step behind him, hoping Diaz would lead the way to the equipment room. He did, pushing open the door to the clubhouse. Felix saw a telephone on the wall and remembered his promise to call his mother. Before he did that, though, he had to make sure he didn't let Diaz get away again. Not without getting some information first.

"*¿Señor Diaz, de dónde es?*" Felix asked.

"*La Dominica,*" Diaz answered.

The Dominican Republic–not Cuba, Felix thought. "*¿Conoces Sammy Sosa?*"

"No," Diaz said, laughing. "*Y, por favor, llámeme Santi. Como se llama?*" He stuck out his hand.

"Felix. Felix Piloto de la Portilla."

"*Ay–de la Portilla–es un nombre bueno por el jugador de béisbol.*"

Felix tensed. If Santi thought de la Portilla was a good name for a baseball player, did that mean he knew his father? How could he ask? He couldn't let on that he was Claudio de la Portilla's son. He was supposed to be the batboy.

He'd choose his words carefully–he asked if Santi ever *played* in Cuba.

Santi grinned. "*Muchas veces. Yo–*"

"Santi!" The clubhouse door opened before Santi could finish what he was going to say. Cookie's head appeared. "Mench wants to see you in his office."

Santi put down the bag he carried in. "*Un momento*, Felix."

Muchas veces. Many times. He had played in Cuba many times. Felix's father would probably be older than Santi, but still . . . They could have faced each other in a game.

Anyway, he needed to know for sure. Maybe Santi had stories about his father's playing–about great catches he'd seen him make, or balls he had hit into the corner. He couldn't go home tonight. He had to find out more. He headed back out to the bus for the rest of the stuff. As he carried in each load, he scanned the room, looking for a place to hide and a spot he could spend the night. When the room was empty, he quickly dialed home.

The phone rang. One ring.

Two rings.

Three rings. The answering machine picked up. Felix heard his own voice saying no one could come to the phone right now. What a relief! Leaving a message would be much easier than having to talk to Mami directly. But what should I tell her? He had to think fast.

Beep.

"Mami, I'm okay. I lost Maryann, so I went home with a friend. I'll call you in the morning."

If he wasn't so scared, he might have laughed. "What friend?" his mother would wonder. But only for a minute. She would quickly realize he had made it up.

Felix hung up the phone and headed toward the bathroom. He made up his mind to hide in a toilet stall. He could pull up his feet so anybody who bothered to look would think the room was empty. The idea of having to sleep outside–even on a warm night–scared him.

"Hey, you made it!" A lanky young man in jeans and a yellow golf shirt came toward him.

"Excuse me?"

"You're the new batboy, aren't you? I'm Bobby Piloto." He stuck out his hand.

The outfielder! "My name is Felix. . . ." He caught himself. He had to stop telling people his full name. "I have relatives named Piloto. In Cuba. Are you from Cuba, Mr. Piloto?"

"No, Piscataway, New Jersey."

"Oh. But your family is from Cuba?"

"A long time ago, I guess."

Diaz came back into the clubhouse and walked toward them. Bobby slung his arm around Diaz's shoulder. "You meet my roomie? Best-hitting catcher since Mike Piazza!"

Diaz winked at Felix. He seemed to understand that English phrase just fine.

But Bobby must have taken the wink to mean that Diaz and Felix knew each other, because next he asked, "Oh, is this your kid, Santi?"

Felix could tell from Diaz's expression that he needed a translation: *"Él quiere saber si yo soy tu hijo."*

It took a second, but Diaz laughed, then shook his head.

Felix asked Bobby, "You don't speak Spanish?"

"Not a word."

"Shouldn't he have a roommate who does?"

"They want him to learn English. Anyway, try to be on time tomorrow, Felix. We had a job for you to do today and everybody was disappointed when you didn't show." He turned to Diaz. "You coming?"

Diaz nodded. It appeared he understood more English than Bobby did Spanish. *"Un momento,"* he said. He took Felix by the arm and led him to his locker. Diaz pushed aside a warm-up jacket hanging from a hook and pointed at a fuzzy color photograph taped to the wall. It was a snapshot of a woman and a boy. The woman's brown arms hung around the boy's neck. They both had bright smiles.

"Mi esposa y mi hijo," Diaz said, but Felix had already figured out they were his wife and son.

Now Felix understood why Bobby had asked if he was Diaz's son. He *did* look like the kid in the picture. The boy had a missing front tooth, and Felix was taller, and skinnier, but their coloring–eyes, hair, skin–was the same. They could've been cookies cut from the same batch of dough, just stretched and shaped a little differently.

"Santi! C'mon!" Piloto called.

"Buenas noches," Santi said.

Felix had more questions, but he didn't get them out. He walked to the bathroom. How could Diaz leave his boy at home? And his wife? Why didn't he bring them with him–especially since he *wasn't* from Cuba? It would be possible for them to leave the Dominican Republic. It wasn't like Cuba, where you had to sneak out in the bottom of a boat or on a raft of half-rotted wood.

He closed the door to the stall and locked it. Was Diaz the last to leave the clubhouse? Felix forgot to double-check.

Where was home for Diaz and Bobby? Did they share an apartment? Felix sat down and wrapped his arms around his legs, pulling his feet up to the toilet seat, trying to picture what a place where minor-league ballplayers lived would look like. They probably weren't home a lot so it was messy, with sports gear everywhere, a comfortable couch, and a big TV. They'd have lots to eat—junk food, and things they could put in the microwave, he bet.

He imagined Diaz's bedside table and saw another photograph there, one he looked at as soon as he woke up. Did Diaz's son miss his father as much as Felix missed his?

Felix thought of his dresser at home, where he kept the baseball his father had hit into the stands, and the photograph Tía Lupe had given him. He wondered: Is there a picture of me on my father's dresser? Does he carry one with him? Show it to the batboy?

Does my father miss me?

Felix knew what Mami would say to that. *He put your future before his own, Felix. That is why we are here. It was our chance.*

Is that what Diaz would say, too? That this was his chance—a chance to play baseball in the Major Leagues?

But what if the answer was no? What if Felix's father never thought of him? Diaz might be able to tell him things about his father's career, and Felix desperately wanted to know all the details. But he wouldn't have the answers to the most important question Felix had.

He turned sideways and leaned his back against the metal wall of the stall. It wasn't exactly comfortable, but it was much better than the luggage compartment.

The lights went out. Felix heard a door close and the jangle of keys. He heard a soft thud, like the sound of a deadbolt notching itself into its rightful place.

Then, silence.

Except inside Felix's head. His mind raced with questions. Tomorrow he would ask Diaz if he knew his father, although Felix realized it wasn't very likely, since he was from the Dominican Republic. But maybe there were other players who really were from Cuba on The Miracle. And he would get to spend the day at a baseball stadium, practically like he worked there! He'd be plenty early enough to see batting practice. He smiled at the thought of the spelling quiz he'd be missing. Then he closed his eyes to the darkness, glad he would be with The Miracle one more day. He needed to be here. He needed some answers.

Maybe this is *my* chance, he thought.

The Miracle

5

Felix woke several times during the long night. He folded his Egrets jersey into thirds to use as a pillow and laid on the carpet by Diaz's locker. He heard an ambulance wail, and a train blowing its horn somewhere in the distance.

But it wasn't the noise that woke him. It was his dream.

Asleep, Felix was still trapped inside the luggage compartment, inhaling bus fumes. He woke twice in a panic, fighting for breath, like he was drowning. He felt cold, but not from the metal of the luggage bin–the cold felt like icy water licking his face. He forced himself to wake up, blinking into the blackness, trying to remember where he was and what time it might be. He realized he'd had a dream like this many times before, but tonight the drowning seemed real. He felt like he hadn't survived the bus ride after all.

When light slipped in under the cracks of the doors and through the windows near the ceiling of the clubhouse, Felix was awake again, his mind full of questions. He wondered if his mother ever regretted leaving her home in Cuba. When he thought about it now, he realized she never said she made the wrong choice. But wasn't she disappointed to have to work so hard just to live in a crummy duplex with a yard that had no grass? Before he started school, he and Mami had shared a room in Tío Toni and Tía Lupe's house in Hialeah. He knew Mami didn't want to go back to those arrangements. She always said how lucky they were to have their own place.

But Mami spoke of her childhood like it was paradise—waking to the cackle of the rooster who lived in her yard rather than the screechy alarm clock that hustled her out of bed now. When she was thirsty, her father would lop open a coconut with his machete and let her slurp out the sweet milk before he cut the white meat into slices. When there was ham, her mother would grind it very fine and make *croquetas*. Mami made these for Felix on special occasions, like *Nochebuena* and his birthday. Thinking about the sizzling hot *croquetas* reminded Felix how hungry he was now. He could eat . . . a baseball. He laughed at the thought, then wondered if there might be food hidden somewhere in the room.

Shadowed light filled the clubhouse. Felix used the bathroom, splashed his face with water, and ran wet fingers through his hair. He wished he had his toothbrush.

He kneeled, resting his elbows on a wooden bench, and folded his hands in prayer. "*Dios*, thank you for letting me live through the bus ride. I promise I will never try that again. Now I need a little help with this next part. Please forgive me if there are any lies. They will be as small as possible." He made the sign of the cross, then padded across the carpet in his bare feet, picked up the phone, and dialed his number.

His mother picked up on the first ring. "Felix?" she asked in a breathless rush.

"*Hola*, Mami."

"Where are you?"

"I went home with a friend I met at the game."

"Felix, what friend? I cannot believe you did this! *Dios mio!* I am ready to kill you! You're not supposed to go home with someone without telling me. What friend?"

"You don't know him. His name is Santi."

"He is Cuban?"

"No, from the Dominican Republic."

"You know him from school?"

"I know him from baseball."

"Ay, Felix. *¡Mi corazón!* I was worried! I didn't believe Maryann that you had left with a friend. I thought she had lost you. I even called the police and had to call them back when I got home and heard your message."

Maryann told her he went home with a friend? She really was as bad as he always thought she was. Felix drifted off into thoughts about what ought to happen to a babysitter who would tell such a large lie. If his mother knew the truth, she would wonder why Maryann had not been struck dead instantly by a bolt of lightning.

Then Felix remembered he was about to tell a whopper himself, so he had to quickly shake off thoughts of how God might punish Maryann. "Mami, *lo siento*," he said, and he *was* sorry. "I didn't mean to worry you. I made a mistake. I should have called you first, but Maryann wouldn't let me. She said it wasn't an emergency."

Mrs. Piloto let loose a stream of Cuban curse words that Felix had heard her say only a few times before. He held the phone away from him in case a laugh burbled out. When she finally quieted, he said, "Don't worry, Mami. I don't expect you to say, 'You were right, Felix. I should have let you go to the game with Jake.'"

"You *were* right, Felix. But, *m'ijo*, these are not the kind of plans you make on your own. How are you going to get to school now? Do you need a ride?"

"No, I'm . . . going to be with Santi."

"This is a nice family?"

"Very nice, Mami—a mother, a father, a son. And, Mami, listen, *por favor*, I got a job for tonight, as batboy."

"No jobs, Felix."

"It's just for this one night, please, Mami. I really want to do this."

"Jobs can wait, Felix."

"Mami, *por favor*. I am begging. Please."

"Felix, you are wearing me out. Okay, but only because it is not a school night. And, to be honest, we haven't solved the problem at work so I will probably be late again, too. Will you need a ride home?"

He was right. Forget about whether my father misses me, Felix thought. If I disappeared forever my mother would barely miss me at all. He was about to get very sad at how easy this lie was going down when he realized it suited his purposes. He could be gone for the whole day, try to get some information about his father, and not have to tell Mami where he was until he did. It was her fault anyway. He wouldn't have gotten on the bus if she had just taken him to the game. And he wouldn't have to find out about his father from strangers if she would just talk about him more. "Can I call you when the game ends? It might be ten o'clock."

"*Ay,* just this once, Felix. You and your baseball dreams. Certainly, you are Claudio de la Portilla's son. No one would doubt it."

Felix found himself without words. His mother rarely even mentioned his father's name aloud anymore. How could he tell her how much it meant to him for her to say he was just like his father? His anger at her from the night before leaked away. Maybe because he was on his own—the first time other than a school trip he had ever been farther from her than the distance between school and her office—but a lump formed in his throat. He missed her. "I love you," he told her.

"*Te amo, también,*" she said, smacking her lips together to send a kiss through the receiver. Felix did the same before hanging up.

"It's your lucky day, lover boy."

Felix wheeled around. A man in sunglasses, jeans, and a white polo shirt stood in the threshold of the door. Felix hadn't heard it open.

"I was just calling my mother," Felix said.

"Yeah, yeah. You're kissing your own mother over the phone.

I'm sure. Anyway, it *is* your lucky day, because Dickey's going to be in court fighting a traffic ticket this morning. Otherwise, he'd be here and you'd be fired."

Felix didn't know who this man was. He also didn't know who the man thought Felix was. And he wasn't sure what he had done to get fired from whatever job he was supposed to have.

All this confusion must have shown up on Felix's face. Before he could get a word out, the guy said: "Aren't you the new bat-boy?"

Felix dug his hands into his pockets. What should he say?

The man took his silence as a yes. He slipped his keys into his shorts and went around the clubhouse, flipping on lights, before he turned back to Felix. "Well, I can see you're sorry. I'll tell Dickey you were extra early today, but that still might not save you from not showing up at all yesterday. He was ready to kill you."

He'll have to get in line, Felix thought.

"I'm here early 'cause I thought *I* was washerwoman for the day, so I'm actually thrilled to see you. How'd you get in here? Was the door unlocked when you got here? Good thing the laundry's dirty, otherwise somebody probably would have stolen it."

The man was talking fast and had many questions, but he was really talking to himself, so Felix kept quiet.

"You know where the laundry room is?" he asked.

Felix nodded, but the man didn't wait for an answer. He walked to the other side of the clubhouse. "Here you go," the man said, opening the door. Felix saw the man's polo shirt had

The Miracle's logo stitched over the heart–a leafy palm tree with baseballs growing where the coconuts should be. The name "Vic" was embroidered in teal thread just below the palm tree. He turned and studied Felix, same as Felix had just studied him. He narrowed his eyes. "How old are you?"

"Thirteen." Felix looked him straight in the eye because once he heard a TV detective say he knew a criminal was lying because the guy wouldn't look at him directly. Anyway, he was almost twelve. A very small lie.

"Isn't there school today?"

"Teacher-parent conferences." Felix looked at his feet. Do small lies add up? How many does it take to make a medium-size lie? He remembered to pick up his head, but the man wasn't looking at him anyway. He was opening the cabinets above the washers.

"Parent conferences, huh? And that was your mother you were blowing kisses to on the phone?" He turned and looked directly at Felix. Felix tried very hard not to react to the man's stare. "You think you can do the laundry without screwing it up?"

"Yessir."

"And don't call me 'sir,' willya? You're making me feel old."

"I'm sorry, sir. I don't know your name."

"Oh, for Pete's sake. I forgot my notoriety hasn't reached middle school yet. Vic–Vic Mench, president and general manager of this mess." He put out his tanned hand. He had a big gold ring on the third finger. Felix recognized what it was right away. He had seen a picture in the newspaper of the one the Marlins got when they won in 2003.

"Wow. A World Series ring?"

"Yeah." Vic held his hand out flat so Felix could get a better look at it. "It was my dad's—he was on the Cardinals team that won in '67. I oughta put it in a case on a shelf—y'know, to keep it safe—but..." Vic turned his hand around and twisted the ring a bit to straighten it on his finger. "On my hand it keeps my dad a little closer. Know what I mean?"

Felix locked eyes with the man. "Yes," he said, "I do know what you mean."

"I know Dickey probably told me your name, but it went in one hole in my head and out the other."

"Felix."

"Welcome to The Miracle, Felix. It's gonna take one to keep this team alive."

"Is the team in trouble?"

"Well, not if you don't count twenty-six consecutive losses to end last season, or that our parent club dropped us as an affiliate, so that not one of my players moved up as a result," Vic said. "Other than that everything's fine. And—hey! We won last night! We're on a roll."

So The Miracle didn't feed its players to any Major League team. "That's like the whole team getting cut," Felix said. "What a lousy way to end the season."

"End the season? Before last night we were winless since July. Florida League record." Vic pulled down a huge box of laundry detergent. "I had the number for the suicide hotline posted by the phone."

"No wonder the guys were so happy last night," Felix said.

"I had a reliever who locked himself in an equipment closet in the eighth inning of one game last August and wouldn't come out until the game was over. He said he couldn't take another loss."

"How many did he have already?"

"Well, if he had taken the *L* in that game, it would've made sixteen."

"Sixteen losses in one season?"

"No. Sixteen in August. He was our closer."

"Is he still your closer?"

"No. He's a roofer now. We got a new closer–and it's a new year, Felix. A blank slate. If we can figure out a way to win this year, who knows, we might get picked up by one of the other Major League franchises."

Vic gestured at the soap. "Here's the detergent. Everything else you need's in one of these cabinets. No bleach on the jerseys . . . but Dickey went over all of this with you already, right?"

Felix gave the slightest of nods. Vic left the laundry room but called back, "If you get bored, I've got tons of mindless chores that need to be done. Homer needs breakfast, for starters."

"Okay." Who was Homer, Felix wondered, and would he eat all his food or would there be some left over? Felix's stomach growled again. He used his fingernails to work at the knot on the laundry bag's drawstring.

"Oh, that reminds me–you like Krispy Kremes?" Vic asked.

"Sure," Felix said.

"I got a dozen on my way in. Can't eat 'em all myself." He had reached the door to the outside. "Actually, I probably could, but

I shouldn't. So come help me finish 'em once you get the clothes going." He saluted Felix and pushed the door open, disappearing into the bright Florida morning.

Felix started two loads–one of pants, and one with The Miracle's bright green jerseys. He left the stinky socks, jocks, and undershirts in a pile for a third load. Maybe whoever was really supposed to be doing the wash will arrive in time to handle those, he thought. "But then I'd be out of a job," he remembered. Felix immediately recanted his wish.

He put in detergent and waited until both machines started filling with water. Then his growling stomach propelled him out of the clubhouse in search of doughnuts.

Outside, a breeze rustled the fronds of the palm trees. Felix's science class had done sundial experiments earlier in the year, and he guessed by the sun's position in the sky that it was not yet nine o'clock in the morning.

He heard Vic shouting excitedly and followed his voice. Through the open office door he saw him on the phone, with his sneakered feet on his desk. Vic's chair was tipped so far back that, every time he laughed, his ponytail knocked some papers off a tall stack piled on the file cabinet behind his desk. There were two other desks overflowing with boxes and folders, but Vic appeared to be the only person who actually worked in the office. Felix stood in the doorway, unsure if he should enter, until Vic waved him in. He pushed the box of doughnuts toward Felix while he continued to talk on the telephone.

"You gotta hear it for yourself. I *guarantee* you will be amazed," Vic said into the phone. He was smiling and waving his free hand around for emphasis. "No, no! Blind since birth."

Who was blind since birth? Felix wondered. Surely not a ballplayer.

"Seven ten on your AM dial, Eddie." Vic took his feet off the desk and sat up straight. "Okay. See you then." He put the phone back in its cradle and looked at Felix. "I'm trying to get the columnist from the *Ledger* to do a story on our new radio announcer."

"The radio announcer is blind?" Felix asked.

"Isn't that outrageous? I asked him if he knew what the field looked like and he told me he can see it in his mind–all except green. He knows the grass is green, but he can't figure out what green is."

He didn't know what green is? When Felix was younger, Mami would give him a cardboard tube from a paper towel roll so he could do his own play-by-play. He would turn down the sound on the TV broadcast and narrate the game, always inserting his father into the lineup. Mami would smile at him while she folded clothes or did the ironing. But Felix couldn't have done it with the TV *picture* turned off, that's for sure. "How does he know what to say if he can't see what's happening on the field?"

"Well, Don's got a partner–two partners, actually, but only one who talks."

"One is blind and one can't talk?" Felix wondered if the third one was deaf.

"Well, the one that can't talk, that's Gizmo. He's a dog. A Seeing Eye dog."

"Oh, I get it."

Vic laughed and then began again. "Anyway, the other partner–the human one–he does the play-by-play. Don is the color guy. He adds all the details and background. They did a demo tape for me and Don has memorized the stats of every guy on my roster. He knows their numbers from high school and from last year. He knows how they did against lefties with men on base, whether they're more likely to ground out or strike out, where they grew up, what they weigh. He's like a walking, talking encyclopedia. He uses all that information to fill out the picture."

Ha! Felix thought. *There's* a good reason to know lots of facts about baseball. He had a teacher last year who told him he was wasting brain space, space he needed for more important things, by filling it with baseball trivia.

"Don't be shy," Vic said, gesturing to the doughnuts. "I've never seen a kid eat just one. You need milk?"

Felix picked another sticky doughnut from the box. He briefly thought about saving it somehow–for lunch. He had only a few coins in his pocket left over from the money he'd brought to the game the night before. "There's milk, too?"

"Help yourself." Vic pointed to a long refrigerated case against the far wall. It looked like the one in the quick mart that held ice-cream bars and sodas. The phone rang as Felix walked to the freezer case and slid the cover aside. It *was* full of ice cream! Drumsticks and vanilla sandwiches, Italian ices in plastic cups and orange Popsicles. There were also dozens of small half-pint boxes of milk–regular, chocolate, and strawberry. He took a chocolate, opened the carton, and drained it while he listened to Vic talk about a delivery of hot dogs. Felix sidearmed the carton into the garbage and licked his lips.

"They must not feed you at home," Vic said, standing up. "Which reminds me. Homer's gonna be hungry. C'mon."

The phone rang again. "Miracle Baseball," Vic said. "He's in traffic court. Try back about two. Either Dickey or Cookie will be here by then." He hung up. "Let's get out of here before it rings again." Vic led Felix out of the office and around the corner, to the gates leading to the field.

"Are you the only one who works here?" Felix asked.

"At the moment, yes. I am president, general manager, office assistant, chief bottle washer, and cook. Until you showed up, I was the batboy, too, so I'm very glad to see you."

"Who wouldn't want to work at a ballpark?"

"That's a complicated question, Felix." Vic unclipped a metal ring of jangling keys from his belt loop. He strummed through them looking for the right one. "They do like to work here, but they don't stay. For instance, my highly competent office manager–a woman whose organizational skills were second only to her patience with my lack of them–went, shall we say, goo-goo over last year's catcher."

"So why did she leave?"

"Because he did. Something to do with his .185 batting average. Anyway, she fell in love with him just as he fell out of love with minor-league baseball. They both moved to Oklahoma to work at a meat-processing plant."

"So that's why you have a new catcher this year," Felix said.

"Right. I spent the winter scouting pickup leagues in the Caribbean and Central America. Santi was the only one willing to take a chance with me. The rest of them are waiting for the scouts with actual Major League connections." Vic finally found the right key, and he twisted it into the lock. "But the same thing happened the year before. That office manager fell in love with my first baseman, and he got called up to Double-A."

"Bad luck," Felix said.

"No, it's my fault. I gotta start hiring ugly office managers. Or married ones." He pushed open the gate and motioned for Felix to go first.

Felix nearly sighed with pleasure as he stepped onto the field. He had never been inside a baseball stadium before and here he was in his second in two days. Vic walked up the third-base line, stooping to pick up a candy wrapper and a sheet of stray newspaper the wind had blown onto the field. Felix trailed him, his head swiveling to take in everything. The Miracle's stadium didn't have the big fancy scoreboard like The Bird's Nest did, but there were colorful billboards on the outfield fence. There was red, white, and blue bunting along the rail of box seats closest to home plate and a banner that said: BLUE REVIEW.

"What's the Blue Review?" Felix asked, pointing. He remembered the players in the locker room mentioning it the night before.

"A bunch of regulars who yell creatively at the umpires. That's what passes for entertainment when you're in the middle of a twenty-six-game losing streak," Vic said.

"Yell creatively?"

"Funny stuff. Like they sing, 'I've Been Studying the Eye Chart,' to the tune of 'I've Been Working on the Railroad,' things like that. I've had to remind them we got kids here, though. Some of the lyrics are PG-13."

Oh, the PG-13 lyrics would be the ones the guys on the Tigers would learn by heart, Felix thought. That was really what the Tigers were about—fun first, baseball second. Felix wished that didn't frustrate him so much. Sometimes he had to remind himself it was good to have fun, even during a game. "What's that thing?" He pointed to a red-and-white-striped pole in the top row of the right-field bleachers, squinting to make sure he was seeing correctly. "It looks like a barber's chair."

Vic nodded. "We're a full-service ballpark."

They reached the bullpen. "Have to do a little harvesting today, too," he said, nodding his head toward something. Felix leaned over the waist-high wall for a closer look. He saw a square grid of tomato plants, tied to stakes, bearing round red fruit. *Completely* round red fruit. The shape and size of baseballs. He was about to ask about them when, from the far corner of the bullpen, a dog emerged from a small house.

"Hey, Homer," Vic said. The golden retriever made his way to where Vic and Felix were standing, his feathery tail swishing behind him. He sat on his haunches at Vic's feet and rested his head against Vic's thigh. Vic scratched his ears.

"You missed me?"

Homer leaned his weight in some more.

"He's your dog?" Felix asked.

"Technically, he belongs to the team. But I love him and he loves me. Homer, this is Felix, the new batboy."

Homer sashayed over to Felix, sat back on his haunches, and leaned his weight into Felix's legs.

"See, he loves you, too. It's easy for him to love because everybody loves him."

Felix scratched Homer's ears like he had seen Vic do. He never had a dog and he wasn't too sure what to do with one.

"His chow's in that locker," Vic said, pointing to a wooden box with a locked lid. "Here's the key." Vic handed Felix the ring by holding the locker key between his fingers. "Better get him a bowl of fresh water, too."

"You don't have one of those big mascots in a costume?" The Egrets had somebody in a suit of white feathers who propelled T-shirts into the stands with a huge slingshot. The bird also did the hokey pokey between innings with little kids, although Felix wasn't sure what that had to do with baseball. It was pretty lame.

"You've never seen Homer in action?"

Felix realized too late that the batboy would probably already know all about Homer. "I–I just moved here."

"This year?"

Yesterday, Felix thought, his pulse rising with his recognition of how quickly he needed to change the subject. "Does he need to go for a walk, too?" Felix knew enough about dogs to know they went for walks.

"Just let him run around the outfield. Watch him, though. He's pretty good about not leaving any presents for the outfielders, but every once in a while somebody puts their cleat down and is very unhappy."

"Ugh," Felix groaned.

"See the pooper-scooper?" Vic pointed at a long metal pole with a blade on the end of it, hanging on a hook behind Homer's house. "If he makes a mistake, that's what you use."

"And then what do I do with it?" Felix asked.

Vic stepped out of the bullpen and headed back down the third-base line. "Toss it behind the tomatoes," he called. "It's excellent fertilizer."

Could that be what makes them so perfectly round? Felix wondered.

Felix filled up Homer's bowls and watched him gobble the food. Homer turned, pulled back his lips, and smiled at Felix with his mouth full. Bits of kibble fell from his mouth.

"De nada," Felix said. He had never seen a dog smile before, but he was sure it was Homer's way of saying *"gracias."*

While he waited for Homer to finish, Felix spied a baseball that had rolled in among the tomato plants. He crouched and leaned in to get it, careful not to touch the dirt, which contained who knew what. He held it up next to one of the tomatoes.

"That's amazing," Felix murmured. It was almost exactly the same size. All of the tomatoes were. Maybe it's because they're grown in a baseball stadium? He would have to ask Mami about this. One of her dreams was to have a house with a garden, because she had always tended a vegetable patch at home in Cuba.

"It is a little miracle to plant a seed, care for it, and have it grow into something you can eat," she'd told Felix. One year for Mother's Day, he saved his money and bought her a dwarf lemon tree from a man who was selling them on a corner Felix passed on the walk home from school. It smelled pretty, but the fruit never ripened. Felix tried one and nearly died, it tasted so bad. He threw the whole tree away one day because every time he looked at it, he felt disappointed.

Homer was busy lapping water in noisy slurps, so Felix stepped onto the outfield grass and tossed the ball high in the air. He wished he had his glove. In the hours after his homework was done and before Mami got home, Felix had thrown a thousand baseballs into the sky, watching them blend with the white clouds, or disappearing in a sharp ray of sun, before plummeting back to earth, landing with a sure thud in his leathered palm.

Felix was lost in that thought when Homer leaped in front of him and snatched the ball as it was coming down.

"Great grab!" Felix couldn't believe a dog could do that. "But don't slobber on it!"

Homer cocked his head at Felix, as if to say, "Huh?" Then he took off running.

"Hey! I was using that–bring it back!" Felix shouted, chasing him. Felix was fast, but he was no match for Homer. The faster Felix ran, the quicker Homer cut and ran the other way. Homer would never be caught stealing a base, that's for sure, Felix thought. Too bad he can't lay down a dead-fish bunt. "Maybe he can," Felix muttered, giving up. Homer did a full circle around the outfield–a victory lap, it looked like to Felix–before returning to drop the ball at Felix's feet. Felix looked down at it, realizing now that what he thought were nicks on the ball's hide were actually teeth marks. It reminded him of something, but he couldn't think what. He picked it up with his thumb and forefinger, trying to avoid getting his hand slimed.

"I get it, *perro*. This is your ball, huh?"

Homer woofed.

"And you play catch?"

Homer woofed again.

"Of course you do. You live at a baseball stadium. Okay." Felix rainbowed the ball and Homer took off like a shot, tearing up a little turf each time he screeched to a halt in the outfield grass to grab the ball in his teeth.

After about twenty throws, Felix decided he better check on the laundry. "You coming with me, Homer, or you want to go back to the bullpen?"

Homer picked up the ball from Felix's feet and trotted back to the tomatoes, where he dropped it, and then nudged it with his nose until it rolled into its hiding spot under the leafy plants. Then he doubled back to Felix.

"Are all dogs as smart as you?" Felix asked him.

Homer shook his head.

"I didn't think so."

Felix put wet clothes in the dryer and started the washer again, tossing in bleach and detergent.

"*Perro*, you want to help?"

Homer sat at attention.

"How 'bout bringing me that pile of dirty underwear?"

Homer laid down and put his head between his paws.

"See. I knew you were smart." Felix filled the washer himself.

The two of them then went looking for Vic, so Felix could find out what else he should do. The office was empty, but the phone was ringing. Should he answer it? Why not? Vic had said to make himself useful.

"Miracle Baseball," he said, sitting down at Vic's desk to reach the phone. Homer leaned himself against Felix's legs, so Felix could pat his head.

"Vic there?" the caller asked.

"He's here, but I'm not sure where. Can I take a message?"

"Tell him his ad's running in tomorrow's *Ledger*, but the classifieds manager said it's against the law to restrict employment to 'ugly or happily married' women only, so I had to take that part out."

"Okay, I'll tell him." Felix scribbled a note on a pad, while Homer lay down at his feet. "This Vic guy is a little whacked, isn't he, Homer?"

Homer barked.

Felix stood and put the note on Vic's chair because there wasn't a clear spot anywhere on his desk. On the wall behind the desk, there were a few framed photos. Felix leaned in for a closer look. One was an old black-and-white of a Cardinals player with his arm around a young boy.

"That's Pops," Vic said, startling Felix.

"Oh, hi. The phone rang, so I answered it."

"You recognize the kid?" Vic tipped his chin in the direction of the photograph.

Felix didn't know much about Will Mench's career, but he knew the most important thing. Will Mench was in the Hall of Fame. "Is it you? Before the ponytail?"

Vic laughed. "Yeah. Long before the ponytail."

"Did you play ball, too?" Felix asked.

"I never made it past Double-A. You a ballplayer?"

Felix nodded. "An infielder." Then, because he couldn't help himself, he added. "My father plays, too."

"Oh, yeah? Around here?"

"No. In Cuba."

"Cuba, huh?"

"He's on the Cuban National Team."

"You're kidding. He must be good. Most of those guys would be in the big leagues if they could play here. What's his name?"

"Claudio de la Portilla." It came out of Felix's mouth before he could stop himself.

"Claudio de la Portilla? The left fielder?"

Felix beamed. "You've heard of him?"

"Felix, are you pulling my leg?" The phone rang, but Vic didn't move to answer it.

Felix stiffened. "No. He's my father. I have a baseball he hit into the stands–that's how he met my mother. She caught it. Well, she didn't actually catch it. It rolled to her feet and she picked it up...."

"But, Felix." Vic stopped. The answering machine clicked on and Vic's voice directed people to call a different number for ticket sales or leave a message after the beep. Vic turned down the volume on the phone and looked hard at Felix. He was giving Felix the look teachers give C students who, out of the blue, score 100 on a math quiz. The kind of look that asked, "Is this for real, or did you cheat?" Felix had gotten this look from teachers because, occasionally, Felix surprised even himself and did get a perfect score on a math quiz.

There was a strained silence. Felix could tell there was a question parked on Vic's tongue that he wasn't sure he should ask. Then his face cleared and Vic said, "Tell you what. I got a bunch of errands to run. Why don't you come help me and then we'll get lunch at the Shack." Vic put his arm around Felix's shoulder. "Deal?"

"Deal," Felix agreed, but he couldn't help feeling that he had made a mistake by mentioning his father.

Homestand

6

They stopped at a sporting goods store a few blocks from the stadium, then went through the drive-in window at the bank. From the pet store, they got food for Homer. At the nursery, they loaded the back of Vic's pickup truck with sod, fertilizer, and mulch. Felix thought it looked like a lot of stuff for the tomato patch in the bullpen, but he didn't know much about gardening. Maybe he could learn and *start* a vegetable patch for Mami—maybe that would be something they could do together, if she could find time for it.

How long would I have to be away to get her attention? he wondered. One day wouldn't do it. How about one week?

How about one whole baseball season?

An image floated into Felix's head. A boxing ring. Felix in one corner. Mami's job in the other. Ring the bell! Felix thought. Let the fight begin! I'll knock out that stupid job in one round!

"Earth to Felix." Vic awakened Felix from his daydream.

"Excuse me?"

"I asked, 'Are you hungry?'" Vic wheeled the car east, toward the beach. Felix rolled down the window so that he could smell the salt air.

Felix was starved, but did Vic expect him to pay for his own lunch? "Not really," he said.

"You sure are an unusual kid. Knows how to do laundry and isn't hungry–that's a rare combination in a teenager." Vic stopped the truck in front of a white cinder-block bungalow.

"This is the Shack?" Felix asked. It wasn't a big house, but Felix wouldn't have called it a shack. It was a neat little place, with a red-tile roof, a front porch with a swing, and a ribbon of Chattahoochee curling from the sidewalk to the front door. What really made it stand out were the flowers. The path was flanked with hot pink impatiens, and there were window boxes spilling purple bougainvillea. An orange tree had dropped its fruit like lumpy confetti on the front lawn.

"No–this is my old house," Vic said, putting the truck in park. "It was where my wife and I lived when we first got married." He shut the ignition.

"Where do you live now?"

"Condo. On the beach."

"Your wife likes that better?"

Vic sat back in the seat with both hands on the steering wheel. He paused before answering. "My wife died. Of cancer. A few years ago."

In the reflection from the windshield, Felix saw Vic turn his head away. "I bet you miss her."

Vic took the keys from the ignition and pocketed them

before turning back toward Felix. There was an uncomfortable silence while Vic looked at him, like he was searching his face for something. "Every single day, Felix. Every single day."

Felix nodded in understanding.

Vic cracked open his door. "You want to wait here? I'm just gonna put the mulch and stuff in the garage."

"I'll help," he volunteered.

At the back of the truck, Vic laid a bag of fertilizer in Felix's outstretched arms, then grabbed the mulch himself.

"Who lives here now?" Felix asked, following Vic up the driveway.

"Nobody. But I keep it up like Abby would have."

"How come?"

Vic set the bag down so he could lift the garage door. "How come? That's a good question." The garage was dark, but tidy. There was a workbench with tools hanging on a Peg-Board above it. The floor was swept clean. Rakes, a broom, and a hoe dangled from a rack along one wall. "I guess it gives me something to do."

"Where should I put this?"

"Anywhere on those shelves is fine." Vic gestured to a spot at the back of the shadowed garage.

Felix slotted the bag into place, next to a spray bottle of plant fertilizer. "Hey, what's the deal with those tomatoes in the bullpen?"

"Whaddya mean?"

"They look like baseballs."

Vic laughed. "Not everybody notices that, Felix." Vic bugged out his eyes and brought his hands up to his face, wiggling his fingers wildly. "They are my own creation," he said in a Dr. Frankenstein voice.

Felix laughed. "How'd you do it?"

"They're hybrids. I crossed two kinds of tomatoes and kept doing it until I got the right size." Vic got a broom from the side of the garage and swept under the workbench. "My wife was a botanist," he said, looking for more dirt to sweep into his pile.

"What's a botanist?"

"A scientist who studies plants."

"Is that why there are so many flowers?"

He nodded. "She planted all of them, but I guess I've made it my mission to keep them alive."

"And that's why you can't sell the house."

Vic leaned the broom back against the wall and picked up a dustpan. "Yeah, I guess that's why."

It was a much nicer house than the one Felix and Mami shared in East Naples. "You could rent it."

"Yeah." Vic dumped the dirt into a garbage can.

"But you're not ready."

"Right." Vic replaced the dustpan on its hook and stuffed his hands in his pockets. "I'm not ready. And I'm not sure I'm ever going to be. It's ridiculous, isn't it?"

"I don't think so, Mr. Mench."

"Call me Vic, Felix."

"Okay."

"You're a good kid," Vic said, and he put his arm around Felix and squeezed him. Then he put Felix in a headlock and gave him a noogie, which made Felix laugh and pull away. "C'mon," Vic said. "I'm starved."

The Shack was a restaurant in the middle of a long fishing pier poking into the ocean. Felix and Vic sat at a wooden table next to a plate-glass window with a view of the beach. The sand below was dotted with people. Felix watched a small boy repeatedly wade too far into the surf. His mother chased him each time, moving him farther back on the sand and out of the way of the waves that crashed in the spot where he'd been moments before.

"What's your pleasure, Felix?" Vic asked when the waitress appeared.

The menu was four pages, covered in vinyl. Felix felt overwhelmed by the choices and nervous about not having any money.

"My treat, by the way," Vic said. Maybe he sensed Felix's hesitation. "I never had any pocket money when I was your age either."

"I'll have whatever you're having."

Vic ordered fish sandwiches with fries and slaw and sweet tea for both of them. The waitress collected their menus and left.

"Mami is saving every penny so we can move to a better place than where we live now," Felix said.

"I didn't know you . . ." Vic started to say something but stopped. "It's just you and your mom at home?"

Felix nodded.

"And she works. What's she do?"

"She runs the Help Desk."

"The Help Desk? Like for homework?"

"No, for people whose computers are messed up–at the courthouse. She calls it the 'Reboot Desk' because by the time people need her they usually have screwed things up so bad all she can do is tell them to turn the computer off and start again."

"That's a whole job? Telling people to restart their computers?"

"You wouldn't believe how often computers mess up. Or how upset people are when they do. She gets calls from people in the middle of the night who've lost their work because their machine froze. People in *tears*," Felix said.

"Crying?"

He nodded. "Crying. She says, 'Save as you go, Felix, save as you go. They're only machines. You can't depend on them.'"

The waitress brought their drinks. Vic asked for lemon. Felix popped the straw on the table so the paper would come off.

"So your mother works full-time."

"And she goes to college two nights a week."

"So that's how come you're here so early."

Felix took a long sip of his tea so he didn't have to answer.

By the time Felix and Vic got back to the stadium, the parking lot held a dozen cars.

"I got some phone calls to make, Felix. You want to take that sod out to the shed beyond left field? The groundskeeper likes to have some on hand before we start a homestand–in case he's got to make any emergency repairs."

"I'll tell him my tip for planting sod."

"What's that?"

"Green side up."

Vic laughed. "Where'd you hear that?"

"TV."

"I gotta remember that one. After you drop that off, go on back to the clubhouse and see if Dickey's here yet. He might have something for you to do."

Felix could hear the sharp cracks of batting practice as he carried the sod to the shed, so he came back after his delivery to watch for a few minutes. He was not anxious to meet Dickey, who still might fire him.

In the batting cage, Jerome Mashburn, The Miracle's third baseman, was taking his swings. Mashburn was as wide as a haystack but not as tall. He had biceps the size of hams and he was using them to pull everything to left field. Felix wished he had arms like that. Hitting was not the best part of his game. In the photograph Felix had, his father's muscles didn't look very big either. Felix figured it wasn't his destiny.

Santi was there, too, standing just outside the cage. He caught sight of Felix and waved. Felix gave him the peace sign. Homer was in the outfield, shagging flies, but he came running in when he noticed Felix.

"*Hola, perro.*" Felix bent down to get his face licked and give Homer a good ear-scratching. "You want to come help me finish the laundry?"

"Hey, don't take him. He's our best fielder," one of the players said.

"If I had my glove, I could help," Felix said.

"Here." Bobby Piloto tossed Felix a mitt. It was too big for Felix's small hand, but it was nicely broken in, soft and well creased in the palm.

"*¡Vaya adelante!*" Santi encouraged him.

Felix looked at the others. "It's okay?"

"Sure," Bobby said. "You've done this before, right?"

"Yeah," Felix said. But never against real hitters, he thought. He ran out to his spot in the infield, nervous but excited.

Felix had played a lot of baseball–first T-ball, then coach-pitch, and now on the Tigers, a junior majors team. He'd never been in the top reading group at school, and he'd made the honor roll only twice, but Felix had always been the best fielder on any team he played on. Coach Drew called him "Eureka," which he said was the brand name of a vacuum cleaner. If a ball came anywhere near, Felix sucked it right up.

Mashburn cracked a few soft grounders right at him–Felix figured he was being nice. He fielded each ball cleanly and tossed them back to the coach on the mound.

"Hey, can this kid start?" somebody called. "He's smoother than you, Wilson." The players waiting behind the cage for their turn all laughed at that. Wilson had started at short against the Egrets, Felix remembered.

The next ball shot off Mashburn's bat like it was coming out of a cannon, but Felix saw it coming and dove to his left, his body nearly horizontal to the dirt, his arm fully extended. He heard the ball thwack into the glove, and he closed his fingers around it before he hit the ground and somersaulted to cushion his fall.

"Christmas!" someone yelled.

"Does he have it?" Piloto asked.

Felix held up the glove and showed the ball, tightly sandwiched in the pocket.

The crowd of players whistled and applauded. One of them gave Wilson a playful shove and said loud enough for everyone to hear. "You better watch out. This kid *should* be starting!"

Felix threw the ball back to the pitcher. He tried to be cool, but he couldn't help smiling.

"What's this kid's name again?" he heard someone asking.

"Felix," Santi said.

"Felix the Cat," Bobby said. "He moves like one."

"*El gato*," Santi said, chuckling.

Felix fielded a dozen more balls, though none as spectacularly as the one the players assured him would've led *SportsCenter*'s Top Ten if somebody had been videotaping B.P. Then he returned the glove and got back to work.

"That was great," he said to Homer, who followed him back to the clubhouse. He realized the players were probably exaggerating about *SportsCenter*, but they all wanted to know how long he had been playing, who taught him to go to his left like that, and told him his grab had been phenomenal.

In the clubhouse, a few players were sitting around playing cards when he and Homer came in. Pitchers, Felix figured. One guy was sitting by himself, listening to something through earphones. Another man was sitting cross-legged in front of his locker, his eyes closed, the backs of his hands resting on his knees. He was softly chanting.

Felix looked at Homer and nodded at the player. "Is he meditating?" Homer cocked his head to one side, as if to say he wasn't sure.

Felix didn't see anybody around who could be Dickey, so he went to the laundry room and ironed the team's jerseys. Then he and Homer distributed them. Felix had the jerseys and pants on hangers. Homer carried the socks in his mouth, dropping a pair in front of each locker.

They were just about done when the door opened. Sunlight washed across the clubhouse floor. In walked an older guy, his black hair combed back and slicked down with goop. He had a cigar clenched in his teeth. He must've just put it out, because even though it wasn't lit, Felix caught a whiff of the putrid odor. The guy wore a polo shirt like Vic's and black shorts. Felix guessed this was Dickey by his lower legs. He was wearing the same kind of white athletic socks, hiked up to his knees, that Felix had seen him in the night before. From the luggage bin the socks were all Felix could see of Dickey.

Dickey took the cigar from his mouth. "Who the heck are you?"

"Mr. Mench asked me to do the laundry. I'm almost done."

"Well, finish it." He put the soggy cigar back between his teeth. "*Mr.* Mench?" he muttered, walking away. "*Mr.* Mench has gone to the great clubhouse in the sky." He stopped and turned back to Felix. "Did Vic tell you to call him that?"

"No, sir." Felix couldn't retreat to the laundry room fast

enough. Maybe things didn't go well with the traffic ticket.

"Is he always like that?" he asked Homer in a whisper.

Homer bared his top teeth and gave a low growl.

"Good to know." Felix didn't want to get fired or sent away, so he had to figure out a way to smooth things over. He distributed the rest of the uniforms, then found Dickey unloading a box of new Louisville Sluggers. The wood aroma from the box smelled so good it almost canceled out the stink of Dickey's extinguished cigar.

"Sir, I finished the laundry."

"What happened to the kid I hired?"

"I don't know, sir. Mr. Mench said to ask you if there was anything you need me to do."

"Yeah. Stay out of the way."

A player in sweats and a cutoff T-shirt came in from the field. "Hey, Dickey, there you are. I can't find my batting gloves. I need Nike; I can't wear Franklin."

"Am I your mother?"

"It's in my contract. It's gotta be Nike."

"Just in case nobody broke it to you, buster, there's not gonna be any TV cameras here. For crying out loud, the radio announcer is blind!"

"I think there are some Nikes in the equipment room," Felix said quietly, hoping not to have his head bitten off. Actually, he knew there were. He saw a whole box of them when he put the bags away the night before.

"Well, get 'em then!" Dickey snapped. "I'm not paying you to stand around looking pitiful."

They're paying me? Felix thought. Wow.

"Dickey, go easy on the kid," the player said.

"Who are you, his agent? Felix, you pull that no-show act again, you're gone. Understood?"

"Sir, I'm not the one who didn't show up. I'm the one who *did* show up."

Dickey took the cigar from his teeth. "Well, where's the kid who didn't show up?"

Felix wondered if Dickey expected an answer. "I don't know. He's not here. He didn't show up."

"What hole did you crawl out of then?"

Felix wished he hadn't tried to defend himself. He certainly couldn't say East Naples. "I was born in Cuba. Is that what you mean?"

Dickey put both hands on his hips. "Are you some kind of wise guy? I don't need any wise guys around here. I got enough trouble with rookies who think I care about their contracts."

"No, sir." Felix said. "I'll get the gloves."

"Good!" Dickey had worked himself into a lather.

Felix noticed Homer had disappeared. Smart dog. He realized it was very possible that the reason the real batboy hadn't shown up had a cigar clenched between his teeth.

After Felix got the batting gloves, another player asked him to find double-A batteries for his CD player. Then Dickey told him to make Gatorade for both dugouts. He was adding water to the powdered mix in a plastic tub when he heard someone call his name.

"Felix the Cat!" Bobby walked into the clubhouse, trailed by a bunch of other guys. Batting practice must have ended.

"Masher," the third baseman said, sticking out his hand. He had thick, crooked fingers and skin that felt like sandpaper. He nearly crushed Felix's hand inside his own. "Great glove work out there."

"Thanks." Felix felt shy about being praised so publicly.

"You the one who didn't show yesterday?" Mashburn asked him.

Ay. He was getting tired of this question. "No, I'm the relief batboy."

That drew laughs.

"You tell him about the bat stretcher?" Masher asked Bobby.

"No, I was just about to. Felix, listen, we almost lost last night because somebody misplaced our bat stretcher."

"Bat stretcher?"

"Y'know—to make the bat longer? What? You've never heard of stretching a single into a double?"

"Sure I've heard of that, but . . ."

"Anyway, go ask the Mini Mets if we can borrow theirs. Their bus just pulled in."

"The Mini Mets?"

"Yeah—from Port St. Lucie. The Mets' Single-A team. That's who we're playing tonight."

"Okay." Wow. The Mets had a great shortstop. Felix always watched them when they were on TV so he could study the guy's moves. He wasn't just good—he had *style*. Felix wanted to have style, too. Of course, this was not the Mets, just their farm team, but still. He had to remind himself not to run.

The visitors' clubhouse teemed with people. Players were getting dressed and there were guys standing around with notebooks and cell phones. Felix finally approached a man dressed in the same kind of casual clothing Vic wore, guessing he might be one of the Mets' managers.

"Excuse me, sir?" The man glanced at him. "The Miracle sent me over to ask if they could borrow your bat stretcher."

The man was writing things on a clipboard, but he stopped and gave Felix his full attention. "Who are you?"

"I'm The Miracle's batboy."

"Where's your uni?"

Felix had forgotten that the batboy always wore a team uniform, just like the players. "They haven't given me one," he said, now hoping they would.

"Are you new?"

"No. I started yesterday."

The guy laughed. "J. D.," he called to another man, also dressed in a polo shirt and shorts. Felix decided this must be the uniform of people who worked in baseball but weren't players. "This kid here is the new batboy for The Miracle. He needs a bat stretcher."

Now a bunch of people turned their attention toward Felix. J. D. stepped forward and put his hands on his hips. "Bat stretcher, huh? Left-handed or righty?"

Felix blanched. He hadn't known enough about bat stretchers to ask that question. "They didn't tell me."

"Tell them we only got a left-handed one, but they're welcome to it if that's what they need," J. D. said.

"Okay." The Mini Mets were pretty nice, Felix thought, if they would loan their equipment to the opponent.

Felix trotted back to The Miracle's clubhouse. Masher and

Bobby were sitting together on a wooden bench when Felix told them what the Mets said.

"Durn it!" Masher said. "We need a right-handed one." He paused and tapped a finger against his gold front tooth. Then he stood and climbed on top of the bench.

"Gentlemen, may I have your attention, please?" The clubhouse quieted. Felix cut his eyes to Santi, who was sitting in front of his locker, watching what was going on. "Felix here is our new batboy. First, let's all give him a hand."

There was a round of applause. Felix studied his shoes.

"Now, you all know we squeaked through that game last night, with Santi carrying us on his back, because our bat stretcher was missing. The bad news is, it's still missing."

There was a chorus of groans.

"There's good news, though. Felix, being the kind of kid he is, has volunteered to go to All Sports and get us a new one in time for tonight's game. Right, Felix?"

Felix wondered how Masher knew what kind of kid he was, but he nodded anyway.

"I'm gonna need a contribution from everybody, even the pitchers," Masher said. "Remember–run support means a win for one of you." The room filled with laughter. Lockers opened. Masher took off his cap and turned it upside down. He went around the room, collecting bills. Then he smoothed out the bills and gave them to Felix.

"Thirty-six bucks, Felix. Stuff it in your pocket," Masher said. "And hurry!"

"I will." Felix sprinted out of the clubhouse and across

the stadium parking lot, heading toward the shopping center where he and Vic had been earlier. He couldn't believe this bat stretcher could be so important when he had never heard of it.

Felix felt tired returning from All Sports, his hands empty. It was only two blocks, but the hot sun—and the humiliation at the store—wilted him. As he plodded across the stadium parking lot, he saw Vic and Dickey near the concession stand. They were talking with a tall kid, who shook his head at something Vic said, then walked away, crossing paths with Felix as he left the stadium.

"Where'd you wander off to?" Dickey asked Felix. "That dang dog is in the clubhouse chewing holes in everybody's socks."

"They sent me to All Sports," Felix said, nodding in the direction of the clubhouse. "For a bat stretcher," he admitted.

Vic let out a howl. "A bat stretcher?!!! You fell for that?"

Even Dickey laughed. Felix wished he could laugh, too, but he didn't like being made a fool.

"The only thing a bat stretcher has ever pulled was somebody's leg," Vic said. "I guess you know that now."

Felix nodded.

"They give you money?" Dickey asked. Felix pulled the wad of crumpled bills from his pocket.

"Hey, that's a lot of dough for a bat stretcher," Dickey said. "You keep that, kid. That's yours." He got in a little golf cart, still laughing, and motored off toward the field, leaving Vic and Felix standing there.

"Who was that kid?" Felix asked, nodding at the receding figure of the tall boy, who had reached the stadium gates.

"That was the batboy Dickey hired," Vic said. "I fired him."

Felix drew in his breath. Had he gotten this kid fired simply by showing up? He was getting sucked into something much more complicated than he first intended.

"What's the matter, Felix?" Vic asked.

"Well, I mean . . . maybe you should have given him another chance?"

"Felix, before last night we hadn't won a game since July 28. There are two big differences between this team and that team. You and Santi. I'm not letting either of you get away. For instance, you'll notice I didn't ask you how you knew there was an opening for a batboy here."

Good point, Felix thought.

"It's obviously fate–Lady Fate," Vic said. "Never underestimate the role she plays in the way things work. As my father used to say, 'It ain't over till the Fate Lady sings.' Now, listen to me. Get into the clubhouse and explain to those guys where their bat stretcher is." He took Felix by the shoulders and looked him straight in the eyes. "Make it good, Felix," he said, winking.

"Can I really keep the money?"

"Of course you can. You earned it."

Felix walked slowly back to the clubhouse, thinking of what he could tell Masher and the others, and thinking about fate. Is this my fate? Mami wouldn't think so. She was doing everything she could to discourage him from baseball. How could she when it was so clear? Baseball *must* be my fate! I didn't really run away. This job called me. The team needs me–Vic said so himself. And I want to be here. This is where I belong. This is who I am. A real baseball player. Part of a real team. A team that cares about the game, not like the Tigers. Most of the kids on the Tigers were more interested in the snack the team mom handed out after the game than in the score.

In the clubhouse, Felix went straight to Masher, who was wrapping his ankle with an Ace bandage. Felix tapped him on the shoulder and then stood up on the bench, like Masher had done earlier.

"Excuse me," Felix said. "I might as well get this over with."

Everyone turned to look at him. He cleared his throat.

"I got the bat stretcher. A right-handed one. It was a beauty, with aluminum clamps. It was the best one they had, so I spent every penny you gave me," he said. Felix saw a couple of the players exchange puzzled glances. "I was almost back here with it when somebody in a Mini Mets uniform, wearing a huge baseball on his head, shot by me like a bullet and stole it out of my hands." Felix squatted down to look Masher in the eye. "So, sorry, Masher. You will have to use your regular bat."

There was silence for a long second before the clubhouse exploded with hoots and howls. Even Masher grinned, showing his gold-capped front tooth. Players came by to shake Felix's hand or knock him in the arm.

"Welcome to The Miracle," one said.

"You got us, kid," said another.

"Felix the Cat, that was a good one," Bobby told him. "You know that was your baptism, right?"

My baptism, Felix thought.

Santi came over next. "*Ahora eres uno de nosotros,*" he whispered.

Now you are one of us.

Felix got a lump in his throat.

He couldn't go home now. He was one of them.

Stretch

7 Two hours before game time Dickey had Felix set up the clubhouse spread–cold cuts, bread, condiments, fruit, a big bowl of pasta salad, bottles of water, a platter of cookies–chocolate chip, oatmeal raisin, and peanut butter.

Santi came over and loaded up a plate.

"*M'ijo, es para ti, también,*" he said, gesturing at the food. Felix nodded, relieved to be invited to eat. His stomach was rumbling again even though he had cleaned every morsel of his restaurant lunch.

Santi sat down at a table, off to one side of the room, and pulled out the chair next to him. Felix took it, watching Santi swallow several forkfuls of salad while he worked up his courage. Before he could lose his nerve, he asked Santi if he had ever played against the Cuban National Team.

"*Sí,*" Santi said, dabbing his mouth with a paper napkin. "*Ellos son adversarios duros.*"

Tough opponents. Yeah, Felix knew that. He sipped his water.

"*¿Por qué, Felix?*" Santi asked.

Felix stared at his sandwich. This wasn't going as he planned. He'd thought he could lob a few questions at Santi like two players would softly toss a baseball to warm up their arms. But as soon as thoughts of his father entered his brain, Felix stiffened with . . . what was it?

Fear. He was afraid.

He took a deep breath. Now or never. He had to know. Did Santi remember a particular player–"*¿Conoces el jugador Claudio de la Portilla?*"

"*Por supuesto, Felix. Todos conocen de la Portilla. Él era una leyenda.*"

He *was* a legend? Felix felt his face get hot. *Was* a legend? That made it sound like his father didn't play anymore.

"Where tree-ples go to die," Santi said, startling Felix.

"Hey! You speak English?"

"*Un poquito.*" Santi held his thumb and forefinger about an inch apart to show how much English he knew. "You teach me, *sí*?"

"*Por supuesto,*" Felix said, but he felt the conversation drifting away from the course he needed it to take. Felix had crept close to something, some truth, and he had to press on. "Did you play against him?" Felix asked.

Santi shook his head. "*Eso era antes mi tiempo. Su cuento es muy triste.*"

Before Santi's time? And what sad story? "*¿Cuál es triste?*"

"*La tragedia. Su pobre familia.*"

A tragedy? The poor family? Felix felt faint.

One of the coaches stuck his head in the clubhouse door. "Santi, they're looking for you in the bullpen."

"*Sí,*" Santi called. "I coming." He winked at Felix.

"Have a great game," Felix told him, forcing a smile.

"*Y tú, también, Felix el gato,*" Santi said, ruffling Felix's hair.

Felix almost threw his sandwich, uneaten, into the trash can, but at the last moment he wrapped it in a napkin and put it in a cabinet in the laundry room. He would be hungry eventually.

He left the clubhouse, needing air. He climbed the grandstand and sat in the bleachers. His father wasn't on the team anymore? Did that mean his baseball career was over? He realized he didn't know how old his father was. Was he a lot older than Mami? Felix's mother was thirty. He had assumed his father was the same age–still young enough to play in the United States if he could get here. But maybe he was older. Maybe he was too old to play.

Or could he have been kicked off the team *because* his wife and son left Cuba? Was that the tragedy Santi mentioned? Mami had told Felix that Cuba wasn't like the United States. People had to do what the government said. And Felix knew that El Duque hadn't *left* Cuba, he had *escaped*. Felix wished for years that his father would do the same–sneak off at night in a boat and head to another island, or right across the Straits of Florida to Miami. But he remembered reading a newspaper article about *why* El Duque fled Cuba. The government had banned him from playing baseball after his brother Livan escaped. He was punished for what his brother had done.

The thought was too horrible for Felix to bear. Did his father lose his wife, his son, and his spot on the team all at once?

Felix looked out over the field, trying to shake the guilt he felt. His mother's words echoed in his ears. *"He put your future before his own, Felix. That is why we are here. It was our chance."* Felix had been carrying this information with him for as long as he could remember. It was heavier than the brick at the bottom of his book bag. He realized he hated it—he wanted it gone. And the way he had always believed he would get rid of it was for his father to arrive. When his father came to Florida, the weight would be lifted. Now he wasn't so sure about that.

He looked out at the field where the groundskeeper was laying down the foul lines with lime. Homer came trotting in from the bullpen, wearing a white jersey that said MIRACLE across each flank, a baseball cap, and sunglasses. He had the handle of a straw basket clamped between his jaws. Felix watched as Homer stopped at home plate, which the umpire was sweeping clean with a brush, and put the basket at the umpire's feet. Felix couldn't tell for sure, but it looked like the umpire gave Homer something to eat from his pocket. Then the umpire took the basket, which was full of dazzling white baseballs, and filled a pouch strapped to his belt with them. When it was empty, he gave the basket back to Homer, who turned and padded back down the left-field line.

"Wow," Felix said aloud to no one. It was almost too much to take in. "That is some dog."

• • •

Thinking had given Felix a headache, so he left the stands and walked back toward the clubhouse.

From a distance, he saw Vic in the concession stand area, talking with a tall guy Felix didn't recognize. The guy handed Vic a yellowed piece of paper from a folder. The tall guy also had a long, narrow notebook and a pen behind his ear. Vic was intent on reading whatever it was the guy had handed him. Felix was only about twenty feet away when Vic lifted his head from the paper and saw him.

"Felix!" Vic waved him over, then folded the newspaper clipping–Felix could see now that's what it was–and put it in his back pocket.

"I want you to meet Ed Foley, the sports columnist for the *Ledger*," Vic said. "We were talking about your dad."

Ed stuck out his hand. "You're Claudio de la Portilla's son?"

Felix shook his hand and nodded his head, but he felt uncomfortable–why? He had told every kid at school who his father was, even some teachers. Nobody had ever made anything of it. He had figured no one believed him.

"Did you just move here?" Eddie asked.

Oh, boy. Now Felix wished he was still in the bleachers thinking thoughts he didn't want to think. How could he get away from this conversation quick? "Yes," he said. "Um, Mr. Mench?"

"Vic."

"Vic." Felix pinched his shirt between his fingers. "Is this what I should wear for the game?"

"Nobody give you your uniform?"

Felix shook his head.

"Get Dickey to tell you where it is."

Felix didn't hesitate. He mumbled, "Okay," and strode away.

"Nice to meet you, Felix," Eddie called after him. Felix turned to wave. Now, the guy was scribbling in his pad. Felix felt sure he was about to be uncovered as a runaway.

"Nice to meet you, too," he said to be polite.

In the clubhouse Dickey grunted and pointed at a rack in the laundry room that held extra uniforms. "Look on the left end–it's gonna be a dress on you."

Felix found a Miracle jersey with the letters *BB* on the back instead of a number. He had time, so he got a towel from the stack and took a shower. There was soap and shampoo in dispensers, built into the shower stalls.

He wished he had thought to toss his own underwear and socks in with the uniforms earlier. And he wished he had his cleats. His sneakers would look stupid with his uniform, which was . . . professional. The pants came with a teal belt that matched the lettering and the stirrups of the socks. His Tigers uniform was really just a T-shirt with the team insignia printed on the front and the sponsor's name–Splasher's Pool City–and a number printed on the back. This jersey was a real shirt, with a V-neck and buttons down the front. The palm tree bearing baseball fruit was stitched on and so was all the lettering. Felix couldn't help but steal a glance at himself in the mirror.

He fit his teal cap with the gold brim onto his head, pulled down low, the way he liked it.

Dickey had been wrong. The uniform wasn't too big. Felix actually felt taller in it–like he had grown in that instant to fill it out.

I look like a real ballplayer, Felix thought. His skin stood out against the sharp white fabric of the jersey. He wished Mami could see him.

He wished . . . he wished his father could, too.

But he never will. It hit him like a punch. He's in Cuba, but no longer playing baseball. He could leave if he really wanted to, but he hasn't. He isn't going to. Ever.

My father is never coming to America.

Felix swallowed hard. It was true. He knew it as well as he knew how far back in the hole you had to position yourself in order to field a one hopper off the infield grass. He knew it in his soul.

My father will never see me play. He will never coach my team. He forced himself to repeat the words in his head.

He . . . is . . . not . . . coming.

I am on my own.

Tears tried to come to Felix's eyes, but he fought them down by correcting himself: No, I'm not alone. I'm part of a team. This team. He gave his head a little shake, adjusted his cap in the mirror one last time, and headed out to the field.

The game was about to begin.

• • •

The uniform made Felix feel not only taller but older, too. Kids asked for his autograph and begged him to throw the balls he was clearing from the field into their outstretched gloves. Felix smiled at them but put the balls in the bucket. The very last one he spun into the air, toward the stands. Kids swarmed underneath it, their gloves opening like flowers to the sun. One kid jumped on a seat and snatched it. The other kids moaned and stamped their feet. The fans who'd already settled into their seats clapped for the boy. Felix was surprised to find himself smiling.

Cookie, the manager, and the players kept him busy–bringing balls to the bullpen, putting away the fungo bats and the other warm-up stuff. He remembered to get a bowl of water for Homer, too.

"In case you get thirsty, from carrying all those balls," he told him.

Homer sat at Felix's feet. He tried burrowing his nose between Felix's knees but the bill of his baseball cap got in the way, so Felix squatted down. Homer moved even closer, nearly knocking him over.

"You need a lot of love, don't you, Homer?"

Homer licked his chin.

"Even more than you need water or food, right?"

Homer barked.

"I totally understand," Felix said, hugging him. Homer wagged his tail.

• • •

Right before the national anthem, Cookie sent Felix to get towels for the dugout.

The clubhouse had emptied. Felix snatched a stack of towels from the supply closet and was headed out when his eye caught the telephone he had used the night before to call Mami. Maybe it was the uniform. It sounded funny to admit this to himself, but it made him feel braver.

He dialed his home number first, but got the machine. Then he dialed the office.

"Help Desk. Connie Piloto," his mother answered.

"Mami, is my father still on the Cuban National Team?" Felix asked.

"Felito—hello. How was your day?"

"Is he, Mami?"

"Felix, really, why are you asking me this now?"

"I'm at the ballpark already and was talking to a catcher here who faced the Cuban team last year, and he said he knew who my father was but he'd never played against him."

"How did you get to the ballpark, Felito? I hope you are not riding the bike all that way. You would have to cross the highway. . . ."

Felix cut her off. "Is he, Mami?"

She sighed. "No, Felix, no. He is not on the team."

Felix took a deep breath to steady himself and pressed his shoulders back, standing straight. He nearly whispered his next question. "Why didn't you ever tell me that?"

"I have tried to tell you a few times, when you were younger,

Felix, but the last time we talked about this you got very angry. You didn't want to hear it."

"When was that?" Felix asked. But he knew—the memory of that conversation flooded his brain.

"*Ay*. Let me think," she said.

"It was in the living room at Tío Toni's house," Felix said.

"*Sí*, I remember. It was right before we moved to East Naples. How old were you then?"

"Five."

"You were about to start kindergarten." Mami let out a big sigh. "I talked to the doctor at that time, Felix, and he said I should stop trying to correct you. He said you were not yet ready to hear what I was trying to tell you."

"Can you tell me now? What happened?"

"*Ay*, Felix, this is not the time to have this conversation, *m'ijo*."

"Well, when is the right time?"

"We can talk about it when I pick you up."

When she picks me up. He couldn't wait that long, although he knew. He was sure he already knew the answer to the question he most wanted to ask. So he just said it. "My father is never coming to America."

There. It was out.

He heard his mother inhale a deep breath. "No, Felix. He is not coming."

Felix leaned his head against the cool clubhouse wall. He closed his eyes. He had so wanted to be wrong, for her to say, "Of course he is coming, Felix."

"Are you still there?"

"Um-hm." It was all he could manage.

"Felito, one of the things I have been trying to get you to understand, something your father never learned, is that there are more important things in life than baseball."

"Like what?"

"Like your family."

"Baseball is more important to my father than his family?"

"No, maybe not." His mother sighed. "But baseball got in the way of him loving his family, Felix."

"Is that why you don't want me to play baseball?"

"I never said I didn't want you to play baseball, Felito. I said there are other things in life you need to think about, too."

"Like what? I don't really even have a family."

"Felix! What are you saying? You have me! I am your family."

"But you're at work. You're *always* at work."

"Felix, without my job, we cannot eat."

"We could go back and live with Tío Toni."

"No. We cannot do that."

"Why?"

"Felix, there is a reason. A big reason. I understand we need to talk about this. I promise we will talk about it when I pick you up. *¿Bueno?"*

"Okay."

"And, Felix. I also understand that you miss your father. You will never stop missing your father."

Never? he thought.

"But I *am* your family. Maybe I have been so concerned with feeding two people and providing for two people that I have forgotten something. You have opened my eyes a little with this *conversación*."

"Forgotten what?"

"Maybe I have forgotten I have to love you enough for two people. And I do, Felix. You know that, *sí?*"

Felix's eyes got watery. He had to get off the phone before somebody saw him. "Yeah, I know that. I love you, too. *¿Hasta luego?*"

"Be good," she said.

As Felix hung up the phone, he sensed something moving behind him. He turned and saw the back of someone–someone in a white polo shirt–slipping out the door.

As he took a seat on the bench, Felix couldn't help but notice that the stadium was now packed. There were people moving up and down the aisles, carrying food and drinks, calling to friends, and talking excitedly to one another. Cookie was at home plate, exchanging lineups with the Mini Mets coach. The public-address announcer was babbling on about sponsors and season-ticket packages.

"Full house tonight," one of the players noted.

"Opening night," somebody commented.

"They all heard about yesterday's win," said another player.

"Get real," Masher said. "They're all here to see the dog."

Right on cue, Homer trotted out to the pitcher's mound with a baseball in his mouth. A man in a T-shirt that said C. C.

Davidson Enterprises was throwing out the first pitch, according to the public-address announcer. He took the ball from Homer, wiped the dog's slobber on the back of his shorts, and threw to Santi. It landed well in front of the plate, but Santi scooped it up and gave it to Homer, who took it back to the guest pitcher, placed it in the man's glove, and then sat at the guy's feet. Homer gave the crowd the same smile he had given Felix when he fed him that morning.

The crowd went nuts.

The Mets went down in order in the first. In the bottom of the inning, Masher hit a double, driving in two runs. But the Mets came right back in the top of the second with a dump single, a perfectly executed bunt down the third-base line, and—POW!—a three-run homer.

Then both pitchers settled down. The middle innings flew. The Miracle pitcher, a skinny boy with a thatch of red hair he swept under his cap between each pitch, found his fastball and retired eleven batters in a row.

"Where was that heater in the second?" Cookie asked, after another Met swished at air and struck out.

"He had it under his hat with all that hair," Felix said. The bench laughed.

Between innings, there was also plenty to keep the fans entertained, and Felix's mind off his conversation with his mother. Homer ran a race around the bases with two kids.

"Does he always let them win?" Felix asked Bobby, because

after taking an early lead, Homer slowed to a trot between second and third, letting the kids get ahead.

"His record is worse than ours was last year," Bobby said.

Then there was a contest between two guys to throw a baseball through a cardboard cutout of a glazed doughnut–blindfolded. Neither came close, but they both got a dozen free doughnuts for trying. Mr. Met toddled out with his big baseball head and tossed balls to Homer, who ran them down and delivered them into Mr. Met's oversized white hands. Homer also gave out autographs–paw prints on a black-and-white photograph of him in his uniform. Kids lined the rails on the third-base side with their hands outstretched to get a picture or pat Homer's head.

"You weren't kidding about people coming to see Homer," Felix said to Masher. They were sitting on the bench, chewing sunflower seeds while The Miracle batted in the sixth.

"That's Vic. He hired Homer last summer so people would come out even when we couldn't buy a win."

"Where did he find him?"

"Hollywood."

"He went to California to get a dog?"

"No, Hollywood, Florida. He was working at a Dairy Barn, bringing people their change in a plastic basket."

"Oh, I thought maybe Homer had been in the movies. I could see it."

"Well, he'll probably move up to The Show before any of us do. If Vic lets him."

The thought made Felix's heart heavy. He hoped Vic would never sell Homer, no matter what.

• • •

The Miracle entered the bottom of the seventh still trailing by one, but Bobby led off by slapping a ball up the middle just beyond the reach of both the shortstop and the second baseman. It dribbled into center field for a single.

The next batter popped up.

"Felix the Cat, c'mere." Masher was in the on-deck circle with Santi, who was up next.

Felix hurried over. "Knock wood," he said.

Felix smiled and rapped his knuckles on Masher's bat. "This won't work. I've never been lucky," he said.

"Batter up!" the umpire called.

Santi had been watching Felix and Masher and now he quickly jabbed his bat between them so Felix could give it a knock, too, before he strode to the plate. "*Gracias*," he said, and trotted off.

Felix watched him take his practice swings, wondering whether Santi's son was a baseball player, too. He was sure he was. Felix could picture Santi teaching his son how to choke up on the bat, how to wait on the pitch, how to put his legs into the swing. He bet the son was home now, thinking about where his father was.

Santi ground his foot into the batter's box dirt and struck his pose. The first pitch came in high and fast.

Santi clobbered it.

Felix leaped from his seat to watch it go—a moon shot over the left-field fence that gave The Miracle a one-run lead.

The crowd erupted. The dugout cleared. Homer raced in

from the bullpen and circled the bases with Santi, which made the crowd cheer even louder. They started chanting, *"Ho-mer! Ho-mer! Ho-mer!"* The players crowded around home plate as Bobby crossed it, holding out their palms for a slap. Santi jogged down the third-base line, his smile flashing against his coffee-colored skin. His teammates smothered him as he scored the go-ahead run.

There was no better moment in life, Felix thought. He collected Santi's bat and slotted it back into place in the rack.

Santi tried to sit down, but Masher pulled him back up the steps to take a curtain call. He waved his cap at the fans. He pointed at Felix, kneeling near the top step of the dugout, and made a knocking gesture with his fist. Felix smiled.

"Maybe your luck's changing, Felix," Masher said to him, handing him the extra bat he'd been swinging to put away.

Felix doubted it.

Nobody scored in the eighth.

In the top of the ninth, the Mets had two batters on with one out. Felix realized he was actually rooting for the Mets to tie so the game would go into extra innings. He didn't want to give up his job as batboy, and he didn't want to make the phone call he had to make, telling Mami where he was.

The next player grounded into a double play.

The Miracle players filed onto the field, shaking hands and thumping one another on the back. Homer trotted out and retrieved the game ball from Wilson, the shortstop. He delivered it to the home-plate ump, then trotted back to the bullpen, his job apparently done for the day. A spray of white fireworks went off behind the scoreboard while the announcer said: "Fans! Come on out tomorrow when your Miracle take on the Mets in a doubleheader. Free Baseball! One paid admission gets you into both games. First pitch at one-oh-five, gates open at noon."

Felix watched from the bench. He felt sad that, tomorrow, he would not be around to see what happened. Could they win three—or even four—in a row? He knew they could.

"What's with the long face, Felix?" Masher asked, striding past him on his way to the clubhouse. "We won!" He slapped Felix on the shoulder but didn't wait for an answer.

Bobby walked by next. "You're our good-luck charm, Felix!" He pulled the bill of Felix's cap down over his eyes and kept going.

The public-address announcer was still talking, cautioning fans to drive safely. Felix went out onto the field, down the third-base line to the bullpen. Through a gap in the outfield fence, he saw car headlights popping on.

As he opened the gate to the bullpen, Homer came out of his house to greet him.

"Hey, Homer—great game," Felix said. "You hungry?"

Homer sat back on his haunches, swishing his tail. He still had his cap and uniform on, though Felix had taken off the sunglasses in the second inning.

Felix refilled Homer's bowls and crouched down to give him a hug. Homer leaned into him, pressing so hard he nearly tipped Felix over.

"So you hug back, too," Felix said. *"Es un milagrito."*

His own words gave Felix a shiver. *Un milagrito?* A little miracle? Where had he heard that before? Was it a word Mami used? He couldn't remember.

Homer licked his cheek, breaking his concentration. Felix laughed. "You want to take off that outfit? You don't sleep in that thing, right?"

Homer whimpered and moved closer, bowing his head so Felix could unsnap the cap. It was fixed on Homer's head with a band that stretched under his chin. Then, he helped him wiggle out of his jersey.

"I'll put this in with the rest of the laundry," Felix told him. Homer wagged his tail again and dug into his kibble.

Felix closed the bullpen gate behind him just as the outfield lights faded and clicked off completely. Dickey was probably getting cranky, wondering where he was, but Felix needed another minute. He climbed into the stands behind home plate.

The scoreboard still lit the grass, giving the field the look of a postcard. Felix took a deep breath, trying to memorize it, but the thought of what was directly ahead of him crowded out everything else. He dreaded the call to Mami, more afraid of how disappointed she'd be than the trouble he'd be in. Although he was definitely in trouble.

He looked across the field at the white lights, rereading the line score. Miracle, four runs on eight hits and no errors. Visitors, three runs on nine hits and one error. Mami had told him his father had played one season—one *entire* season—without making an error. In the Major Leagues, that would have earned him the Gold Glove. It was at this moment that Felix realized what he was truly dreading–the conversation about his father Mami had promised they would have *later*.

Later was fast approaching.

Felix felt an intense urge to run away from it as fast as possible–as fast as Homer chasing a ball in the outfield, as fast as a ball coming off Santi's bat headed for the parking lot beyond the left-field wall.

Just then, Felix heard noises behind him–the snuffling of a dog and the *tap-tap-tapping* of a stick. He turned and saw a sandy-haired man being led by a dog down the steps from the press box. He wore dark glasses and carried a black cane with a white tip. This must be the radio announcer, Felix thought.

"Whoa, Gizmo!" the man said. The dog was straining to reach Felix.

"Hi–it's me, the batboy. He probably smells Homer. I just fed him."

"You're Felix?"

"Right."

"I'm Don, and this is Gizmo, my partner. Well, one of my partners." Don laughed a little. "He's already getting acquainted, isn't he?"

Don was right. The dog had nudged his nose right into Felix's lap and sniffed up and around. "Nice to meet you, Gizmo." Felix scratched him behind the ears.

"We heard about the bat stretcher," Don said.

"You did?" Felix was surprised.

"Yeah, Vic told us. He loves a good story. He told us about

your speech, too. You really turned the tables on them. Was that Vic's idea?"

Felix shook his head, before realizing that wouldn't help Don understand his answer. "Sorta," he said quickly. "I mean, he and Dickey told me I could keep the players' money, but I felt like I had to come up with some explanation."

"Most kids couldn't think that quick."

Felix felt a little embarrassed by the praise, so he changed the subject. "I didn't get to hear your broadcast tonight, but when I was little I would pretend to do the play-by-play for my mother."

"I did that, too."

"So you always wanted to be a sports announcer?"

"For as long as I can remember."

"Wow. I hope this isn't a weird question, but do you know what the field looks like? Where first base is and the pitcher's mound?"

"Yep. I've walked it and touched it and smelled it. People make a big deal over me being blind, but I've never been sighted, so that's about what other people think I'm missing, more than what I feel."

Felix nodded. "I never thought about it that way," he admitted.

"The way I think is, you can't miss something you've never had." Gizmo started to strain on the leash again, trying to lead Don down the steps. "You'll see me tomorrow?"

"Sure," Felix said.

"'Cause I won't see you!"

Felix laughed. "Good night," he called.

"'Night now."

Felix watched Don and Gizmo make their way out to the field, where Gizmo watered the grass. Don's words echoed in the night air: You can't miss something you've never had, he'd said.

Oh yes, you can, thought Felix. *Yes, you can.*

Last Licks?

8 "Mind if I join you?" Vic asked.

Felix had been leaning back in his seat, looking at the stars. He heard footsteps approaching but didn't budge until he heard Vic's voice. "Hey, Vic," he said, sitting up straight. "Great game, huh?"

"Another *W.* Gotta love that." Vic unfolded a seat and eased himself into it. He was quiet for a moment. "Felix, I got two, no, three things to tell you. First is, we have never had a batboy here who did a better job than you did today."

"Thanks." Felix might have enjoyed the praise more, but he had a feeling it was Vic's way of softening whatever the second and third things were he had to say.

"Second thing–and this is more important–I told you a fib today, and I need to set the record straight."

"*You* told a fib?"

"About my wife."

"She's not really dead?"

"I wish." Vic leaned forward, resting his arms on his legs. He was quiet for a while. Felix could see only Vic's profile, but he saw one thing clearly—a tear spilled from the corner of Vic's eye. "No, she is dead, but I told you she died a few years ago. Actually, she died nine years ago." Vic turned his head and met Felix's eyes.

"I wouldn't even count that as a lie," Felix said.

"I've gotten into the habit of not saying how long it's been because I'm so tired of people telling me I should have gotten over it by now."

Felix nodded in the darkness. "I'd do the same thing."

"I figured you would understand. Whatever way you deal with losing somebody is okay. It has to be." Vic wiped his cheek with the back of his hand. "But I should've been straight with you."

A tear welled up in Felix's eye, too. There was a long pause, a deep silence that, like the night sky, went on forever in its blackness. Felix found himself wishing Homer would come by so he could bury his face in his furry neck. He wouldn't even mind if Homer licked him. Yesterday, he would have thought a dog licking him was kind of gross. Tonight, he wouldn't even wipe off the slime. If he ever got out of trouble with Mami, he would ask if he could have a dog.

Mami. He remembered the telephone conversation. He had a confession to share with Vic, too. "My father is never coming to America," he said. "He will never play baseball here." It was a statement of fact, as clear and unarguable as the runs, hits, and errors recorded in the scoreboard lights. It hung in the air like a towering fly ball that refused to come down.

"Were you counting on him coming some day?" Vic asked finally.

Felix struggled to get the words out. "I guess so." His throat had gotten dry and tight.

"Well, that brings me to the third thing, actually." Vic took off his glasses and wiped his eyes with a handkerchief from his back pocket. "You don't live around here, right?"

Felix never considered lying. "No."

"You live in East Naples, right?"

"Right."

"You run away from home?"

"Not really. I called my mother. She thinks I'm with a friend."

"Hey, technically, that's not a lie either. I'm your friend." Vic shook Felix's knee. "How'd you get here?"

"I hid–on the bus."

"Okay. Cookie figured that out. You sleep on the bus last night?"

Vic had talked about this with Cookie? Felix didn't like the sound of that. "No, in the clubhouse."

"Where you sleeping tonight?"

"I guess I better call my mother."

Vic sat up straighter. "Okay, listen, Felix, the third thing is–and I hope like heck you and I are still friends after I tell you this–will you promise me?"

"Sure."

"Good. That's important. I want to stay in touch. Okay, the third thing is I called your mother already."

"You did?"

"Yeah. I asked Eddie–y'know the reporter from the *Ledger*? He tracked her down. Both of us know who Claudio de la Portilla is and neither of us thought his famous kid lived around here."

"Oh." Felix said glumly. He hadn't thought of that.

"She's not mad, Felix. She's relieved you're okay. Although she might be mad tomorrow. Tonight, she's thankful you're okay."

"I'm not too worried about her being mad," Felix lied.

"Actually, she's not mad. She's furious."

Felix winced. "Really?" Would she make him quit baseball now? She had once threatened that when he got a C in English.

"At me. She's furious at me."

Felix laughed. "At you?"

"Yeah, me. I told her she couldn't have you back."

El Milagrito

9 "This is actually more of a favor to me than you, Felix." Vic unlocked the front door to his little house and flipped on the lights. "I haven't spent a night here in nine years."

The inside of Vic's old house was every bit as neat as the outside. It reminded Felix of the model home at a new housing development he and his mother took a tour of right after they moved to East Naples. He knew that was the kind of place his mother had in mind when she put her extra dollars in the drawstring pouch that held their "new house" fund.

He followed Vic through the living room, down a corridor, and into a bedroom. Vic flicked another switch. Felix saw a bed with a flowered coverlet and a white dresser.

"It's a little froufrou, huh?"

"It's better than the floor of the clubhouse."

Vic laughed. "True."

"I'm surprised my mother went along with this."

"I didn't give her a choice. I told her I'd call her in the morning to tell her how to get here."

"She'll probably call the police."

"Nah. I'm good with mothers. Some of my players are only a few years older than you. I've smooth-talked the worries out of mothers who were a lot more tightly wound than yours, Felix. You don't give her enough credit."

"What do you mean?"

"I mean, she understands she's screwed up a little. She said she should have gone to the Egrets game with you."

"She did?"

"Yeah, she did. So you're not going to hold that against her forever, right?"

"No, but . . . the game, I mean–that's not the only thing."

"I'm sure you wouldn't have taken that bus ride if it was. Look–I don't know the whole situation, but I know a little about you and it seems she's done a pretty good job raising a son, all by herself. That's not exactly high cheese on a three-oh count, Felix."

Right. He was right. "I know."

"You could probably cut her some slack."

Felix nodded.

Vic had a gym bag over his shoulder and he unzipped it, producing a Miracle T-shirt. "Your pajamas. There's probably nine-year-old toothpaste in the bathroom, but no toothbrush."

"That's okay. I'm not planning on kissing anybody."

Vic laughed. "Oh, yeah. I meant to apologize for something. Turns out you really were blowing kisses to your mother through the phone this morning. Who woulda thunk it?"

Felix chuckled as he stepped into the room, taking off his cap. He placed it on the shiny top of the white bureau, which made him think of his dresser at home. His dresser had a long nick on its top, which was probably why somebody had put it out as garbage in the first place. He liked the nick, though, because the groove kept his father's foul ball from rolling off.

"You ready to hit the hay?" Vic asked.

"I'm beat," Felix admitted.

"Will it keep you up if I turn on the tube? Takes me a while to chill out."

"Does it feel weird to be staying here?"

Vic looked around the room, like he hadn't seen it before. "I needed to do it, but I needed a reason. See? Lady Fate working her hand again. If you hadn't shown up, I might never have done this on my own."

"Glad to have done one good thing."

"C'mere, Felix." Vic motioned for him to come, so Felix shuffled his feet toward the door. Vic met him and gave him a hug. "You've done a lot more than one good thing, Felix. Anybody can see that." He let him go, but rubbed his head. "You got some bad hat hair, there, *compadre*."

Felix smiled and ran his fingers through his hair, trying to unglue it from the sides of his scalp.

Vic backed out of the room, pulling the door closed with him. "Get some sleep, slugger. Long day tomorrow–free baseball."

"Really?"

"Really. Doubleheader against the Mets. One-oh-five start."

"But I mean, am I really going to the game, or is my mother picking me up first thing?"

"Still to be negotiated. She's anxious to see you, but I'm working on her."

"Okay."

"'Night now," Vic said, pulling the door shut.

"Vic?" Felix called.

Vic's head popped back in.

"Thanks."

"*No problema*, buddy."

Felix folded his uniform over the end of the bed, wondering if he'd ever get to wear it again. He shrugged into the long T-shirt and peeled back the bedspread, slotting himself into the cool space between the tightly fitted sheets. He meant to think over what Vic said about his mother knowing she had screwed up, and how he had to give her more slack, but before he could, he was gone.

Vic was up and dressed by the time Felix got out of bed. It was the sound of the shower that awakened him, but he waited until he was sure Vic had cleared out of the bathroom to get up.

"Morning, Felix. I'd offer you breakfast, but it'd be edible flowers. We'll stop for Krispy Kremes."

"You call my mother?"

"Yep."

"What time is she coming?"

"Not sure, but I told her you were working today."

Yes! Felix thought. "What'd she say to that?"

"She said you weren't old enough to be working—even on a Saturday—and did I know there was a message on the answering machine saying you were out of school illegally yesterday."

"Oh."

"So much for teacher-parent conferences. You want to shower

here? There's soap. It's nine years old but"–Vic smelled his armpit–"surprisingly effective."

Felix laughed. "No, I'll do it at the clubhouse after I put some of my stuff in with the laundry. I didn't bring anything with me when I left East Naples."

"What are you saying, Felix?"

"I wasn't planning on going anywhere but to the Egrets game, so I mean, I don't have clean underwear or socks or anything."

"You mean you've been wearing the same Jockey shorts since Thursday?"

Felix laughed. "Well, yeah, I mean . . ."

"Oh, this is way too much information. Let's go." Vic fit his cap over his head, then opened the front door. He stepped back to let Felix go through first. "Another beautiful Florida morning, Felix, and we got not one, but two, count 'em, *two* baseball games today. Life does not get any better than this."

Felix found a stack of compression shorts in the laundry room, so he tugged on a pair of those before tossing his own stuff into the washers with a big load of dirty stuff from the night before. Then he went to the bullpen.

"Buenos días, perro." He stooped to scratch Homer's ears and the dog almost knocked him down, burrowing into Felix's chest. "I think you're lonely out here, Homer."

"No dogs allowed in the condo," Vic said, appearing at the bullpen fence.

"He needs a boy." He gave Homer one last squeeze before crossing to the locker for the chow.

"And a boy needs a dog. But this one's taken."

Felix filled Homer's bowl and returned the bag to the locker.

"Here–catch." Vic threw him a glove. "Let's toss a few."

Felix trotted behind Vic to the outfield grass. "I thought you said we had a lot to do this morning."

"What the heck kind of ballplayer are you? You're objecting to a game of catch?"

"I'm not objecting...."

"The way I look at it is, what in the name of the Bambino is the good of working at a baseball stadium if you don't take advantage of it? This is practically job-related. Warming up our arms." Vic rifled him a throw.

"My coach says that, too." Felix fired the ball back.

"Does he work at a baseball stadium?"

"No. He said it when he was teaching us to kiss baseballs."

"Oh, man, I love baseball, but I draw the line at kissing them. Tell your coach to get a girlfriend. Or, at least, to kiss his mother."

Vic lobbed a high one and Felix, laughing, lost it momentarily in the sun. When he got the mitt under it, he fired it back, and found himself wondering: Who would he miss more next week, when he was tossing a ball into the air by himself again–the man or the dog?

His next thought scared him: I can't go back to that.

But I am. I am going back. Today. Mami is there and she needs me. I know that.

Still, he felt an ache.

• • •

Because of the one-oh-five start, warming up his arm was the only leisurely moment Felix had all morning. Everything he had to do to get the clubhouse ready the day before had to be done in half the time today.

By the time he finished, it was time to dress. He was buttoning his jersey when Dickey found him.

"Field needs to be cleared, Felix."

He knotted his laces and found a bucket in the dugout to pick up the balls from batting practice. The "ball rats," as Vic had called them, were already in the stands, trying to get his attention. Felix ignored them again until he grasped the last stray ball, which he twirled into the air above the box seats along the third-base line. He watched to see which lucky kid would grab it. A long brown arm reached into the cluster and snatched it.

Mami.

She held it up, a thin smile on her face.

"Not fair, lady," one of the kids said.

Felix ran over to the railing. "Nice catch."

"Thank you," she said, walking down to meet him. "But I have one of these already. If I give it back, will you buy me dinner? I mean, now that you have this big job . . ."

Felix thought of the money he had gotten to buy the bat stretcher. "Sure, I'll buy you dinner."

His mother whistled, attracting the attention of the boys she had bested for the ball. She threw it softly into the air, inciting a mad scramble, then turned back to Felix. "You look *muy guapo* in that uniform, Felito. Very grown up and well, like your father."

"You're early." He was happy to see her, but . . . "Do I have to go change right now?"

"No, no," his mother said, fanning the air with her hand. "I bought a ticket. I am going to watch the game."

"Really?"

"How else do you think I got in here?"

"You don't have to work?"

"Not today. Today is for baseball. My seat is right up there. Will you wave at me?"

"Sure." He felt awkward. There was so much he wanted to say that couldn't be spoken across this railing. "I'm glad to see you, Mamacita."

"And I, you, Felix."

"I thought you would be ready to kill me."

"The thought has crossed my mind several times in the past thirty-six hours."

"I'm sorry." He lowered his voice to a whisper. "I didn't mean to do this. I was so angry at Maryann, and then I got here–and, well, you'll see why I didn't want to come home. Wait till you meet Homer."

"Who is Homer?"

"The mascot. Mami, when we get home, can I get a dog?"

She rolled her eyes. "Don't push it, Felix."

During the game, Felix pointed out his mother to Santi, Masher, and Bobby.

"The one in the red top?" Bobby asked.

"The one waving at me," Felix said.

"That's your *mother*?" Masher asked.

"Wow. She's better-looking than Mench's last office manager!" Bobby said, knocking Felix with his elbow. "You were holding out on us, Catman." He waved back at Felix's mother. She put her hand down.

The game was another close one–no scoring at all until the sixth inning when The Miracle scored two. The Mets came back in the top of the seventh with one run. Felix noticed Vic standing next to his mother during the seventh-inning stretch. For the rest of the game, he kept peeking up at her seat. She and Vic talked throughout the eighth and ninth. Felix wondered what they could possibly be saying to each other.

Between games, Vic found Felix in the clubhouse.

"Felix, after you get the dugouts ready, I want you to take the rest of the day off," he said. "Here." He handed him a program. "Teach your mom how to keep score."

"You sure?"

Vic nodded. "Dickey is getting too used to having competent help. He might soften up."

"But what about when they need towels? Who'll pick up their bats?"

"Hey, I don't want you to go either, but . . ."

"But my mother."

"Yeah. Your mother. I'd love for you to stick around." Vic put his hand on Felix's shoulder. "But it's no fun watching a baseball game alone."

"Okay." He began to unbutton his jersey when Vic stopped him.

"Keep the shirt, Felix. You earned it."

Felix wanted to hug Vic but he felt shy. He did it anyway, throwing his arms around him. "Thanks," he said. "Thanks for everything."

Vic squeezed him back. "*De nada*."

"Hey, that's like the second or third thing you've said in–do you speak Spanish?"

"*Un poquito*," Vic said, holding his thumb and forefinger an inch apart to show him how much Spanish he knew.

Felix got two sodas, a bag of peanuts, a hot dog, and a sausage-and-peppers sandwich before he climbed the stands to where Mami was sitting.

He showed her the tray. "You can choose–the hot dog or the sausage."

"What a feast," she said, lifting the hot dog in its paper slip from the tray Felix held out. "I was only teasing you about buying me dinner."

"How'd you like the first game? That's the third win in a row."

"Your friend, Vic, thinks you are his *encanto afortunado*. He wants me to leave you here."

"Will you?"

"You are very persistent, Felix."

Felix took a bite of his food. His eyes scanned the field and picked up Homer, trotting in from the bullpen with a new basket of balls for the umpire. "Look." He nodded in Homer's direction.

"*Ay,* Felix, you were right about that dog. He is *un milagrito*. I have never seen a dog that could put his paw over his heart like he did for the American song."

"*Un milagrito*–I called him that, too. It fits with the team. A little miracle."

"That's what they called you when you were little."

Felix shook his head. "Really? Why?"

"Because of the baseball–the one your father hit that rolled to my feet."

"I don't get it."

"Do you want to have the talk about your father now, or do you want to wait for the ride home?"

It wasn't that he'd lost his nerve. Felix still had questions he wanted answered. But he had a feeling that as soon as he and his mother had this conversation, his adventure was over. "Vic told me to teach you how to keep score."

"Okay, we can do that first."

So Felix and Mami watched the game intently, Felix explaining how to fill in the boxes to keep the pitch count, how to trace the batter's path around the bases with a pencil mark on the small diamond next to each name. His mother caught on quickly. By the time The Miracle scored four runs in the bottom of the fifth, she was doing the scoring herself.

"How do you mark which player gets the credit?"

"You mean the RBI? Let me borrow the pencil."

She handed it to him.

"For every RBI, put a little dash through the diamond–like this." Felix drew two short straight lines across the diamond next to Masher's name. He had just hit a single that drove in runs three and four.

"It is like accounting."

Felix remembered that Mami had taken a course in accounting at the community college the year before and gotten an A. "Really? Accounting must be okay, then."

"Maybe you can be an accountant when you grow up."

"You are very persistent," he said in a singsong voice, imitating her. "Maybe you forgot? I am going to be a baseball player."

Vic came to visit, bringing them both Miracle baseball caps. Mami threaded her dark ponytail through the back of hers. Vic also gave her an envelope.

"What is this?"

"Felix's wages."

She opened the flap and counted the bills with a long fingernail. "There is one hundred dollars here!"

"It's a week's pay. He'll owe me the rest."

"You can put it in the new house fund," Felix told her. He still had a twenty in his pocket.

Mami folded the envelope in half. "How about the *college* fund—so you can study accounting." She took a sip of her soda. "I know what you two are doing. I did not fall off the sugarcane truck yesterday."

Felix tried to look innocent.

"What are you accusing us of, Mrs. Piloto?" Vic winked at Felix.

"It is ridiculous to keep this up, because our house is in East Naples, my job is in East Naples, and Felix's school is in East Naples."

"But my job is here!" Felix said.

"That is where you are mistaken, *m'ijo*. Your job is going to school."

"She's a tough case," Vic whispered to him. "I'll keep thinking."

They had begun the doubleheader with the sun almost directly overhead, like a spotlight bearing down on them. Now, as the second game was ending, it settled over the outfield fence, coloring the horizon with streaks of orange and pink. Bobby caught the last out–a line drive to right that he dived to grab.

The Miracle won its fourth in a row. The crowd stood on its feet to applaud. Fireworks shot into the air behind the scoreboard again, this time competing with the sunset for brilliance. The loudspeakers blared with the song "We Are the Champions of the World," which if not quite the truth, did match the mood on the field, where the team hugged and slapped hands as if some big title had been captured.

"Maybe you *are* their lucky charm," Mami said, sitting back in her seat.

Felix smiled, but he still wasn't feeling especially lucky. The crowd streamed out behind them. Felix sat down, too. "I guess I'm ready."

"To talk about your father?"

He nodded.

"Okay." Mami took a sip of her soda. "There are a few things I left out of that story I have told you so many times."

"About the foul ball?"

"No, about the voyage from Cuba." Mami smiled at Felix. "Every time we have ever talked about this, you have sat on my lap. But now you are too big for that, no?"

"Shh, I work here."

She smiled at him, then took in a big breath. "The night we left from Cojimar, it was like this night–dark and warm. Beautiful. We had to sneak down to the beach, be absolutely quiet, and wear dark clothing so the moon wouldn't show us. When we got there, there were maybe twenty-five, thirty others, waiting to get on the boat."

"But you told me before there were thirteen people."

"*Sí.* That was the problem. There was actually room on this boat for maybe six people. And all of the people on the beach had already given their money."

"So how did they decide who got to go?"

"Okay, here begins the part I have left out before, but which I think you are ready to hear, no?"

"Keep going," Felix said.

"All along, your father intended to come with us that night. He had had other chances to defect, traveling with the team. But he didn't want to be in America and have us in Cuba with no way then to get us out. And once he had defected, it would have been almost impossible for us. We would be watched, as well as punished."

"We would still be there."

"Correct. Now, the captain of this boat was only too happy to take Claudio de la Portilla–and his money–but the person he absolutely positively didn't want to take was *you*."

"Why? What'd I do?"

"He didn't want any babies. He was insistent."

"What's wrong with babies? A baby hardly takes any space at all."

"That's true, but babies are trouble, Felix. They cry and ... this is the hard part of the story for me, Felix. They can't swim. Which turned out to be important."

An image came into Felix's head. It was the dream he'd had the first night away, when he was sleeping on the clubhouse floor. The blackness, the coldness of water against his skin. "So what happened?" he asked, but he had an idea that he already knew.

"Claudio said, 'He gets MY place. And you will take them'—meaning you and me—'or you will take no one.'"

Felix leaned his head back and closed his eyes, trying to picture the scene on the beach. His strong father. His pretty mother, carrying a baby. A baby who was him.

His mother continued. "The captain finally agreed. Your father is a big star in Cuba. This puny captain couldn't refuse Claudio de la Portilla."

"So we left him there?"

"Him and a dozen others. He promised he would follow."

"But he never did." Felix put his feet up on the seat in front of him and wrapped his arms around his legs. He stared out at the field.

"He never got another chance, Felix, because ... because of what happened. Because of the fuss."

"What fuss?"

"So we traveled for several hours—you were *perfecto*, Felix, not a peep out of you—but then we hit something, something in the water, rocks maybe, or debris of some kind. I never learned what it was. Water started coming in where all of us were hiding, so we went up the steps. The captain started screaming at us to go back down. He was afraid we would be detected."

"Detected?"

"By the Americans—by the Coast Guard. It was illegal, what we were doing. If you make it to Miami, they will take you as a refugee. You know that word?"

Felix nodded.

"But if they catch you in the water, they send you back to Cuba," Mami went on. "Anyway, there were life preservers on the boat, but not enough." She stopped and squeezed Felix's hand. "Is this too much for you?"

"No, don't stop."

"We got one life preserver. One for you and me—because the others knew there was no way I could try to float and hold you."

"And because of who my father was."

"*Por supuesto*, Felix. Even facing death, Cubans think about their baseball stars." Mami reached into her purse and took out a tissue. "We were not allowed to bring anything but one small bag with us, but your father had put his baseball shirt—one of his jerseys from the national team—*muy importante*, this particular shirt—into my bag before we left. He wanted you to have that. So now the boat is sinking." Mami stopped and looked around. The seats on every side were empty, but she lowered her voice anyway. "I buttoned the shirt over the life preserver, so I could lay you on top of it. By this point, you were crying, but so were a lot of people. The rest of my bag went down with the boat, but I took our famous baseball–that foul ball you have on your dresser–and I put it in your hands. And that calmed you. Those little marks that look like cuts? Actually those marks are from your teeth. You chewed on the ball to soothe yourself."

"Wow. Just like Homer's ball."

"Homer chews on baseballs, too?"

Felix nodded. "He keeps one under his tomato plants."

"Homer has his own tomato plants? This *perro* is magic, I think."

"The tomatoes are Vic's, but they are kind of magic. They're the exact same size as baseballs."

"You will have to show me that, Felix. Anyway, maybe chewing on a baseball is soothing to all creatures."

Felix looked at his mother. She was shredding a tissue in her fingers, but her eyes were dry. "Were you scared?" he asked.

"I am more scared thinking about it now than I was at the moment. I was too busy trying to stay alive to be scared then. Are you scared?"

"No. Not really. How come you never told me about the boat sinking before?"

"I worried it was too much for you. I mean, Felito, I have tried to tell you many times that your father was not leaving Cuba, and you . . . you haven't been willing to accept that. I didn't think you were ready to hear about the ordeal we went through to get here. I worried for years that you would be deathly afraid of water."

"Did we float all the way to Florida?"

"Two fishermen saved us. They took you out of the water with a big net on a long handle. And then one of them dived into the water and dragged me to their boat. The other pulled me in."

"And they took us to Miami?"

Mami nodded. "But first they called the Coast Guard to tell them what happened, and we circled around the area, searching for some sign of the others. We found a few things–personal things that belonged to the people. That was more terrifying than anything. Looking but not wanting to see what we might find."

"Did anyone else from the boat live?"

"Two others. They also had the life rings."

Both of them were quiet. A plane soared overhead, lights on its wings winking against the black sky. "So that was the 'fuss'?"

"No, no. The 'fuss' was that baseball." Mami's eyes were now watery and she had gotten a second tissue to blow her nose. She took a deep breath before returning to her story. "When we got to Miami, to the Coast Guard station, someone from the newspaper took a photograph as they were taking you off the boat, and you were still clutching the ball in your hands. That picture was everywhere the next day. And then on the radio, on the talk shows–they started calling you '*el milagrito,*'" Mami said. "This was before anybody even knew who your father was. After it came out that you were Claudio de la Portillo's baby, they wouldn't leave us alone. There was a time when poor Tío Toni couldn't even get his car out of the driveway because the big vans from the TV stations had clogged up the whole street."

"I think I remember that. That's not possible, is it? But today, when I called Homer '*milagrito,*' it sounded so familiar."

"Oh, you have heard it before. All those years we lived with

Toni and Lupe, you were '*el milagrito*.' The boy who lived. Even after the TV people moved on to the next thing, strangers would ring the bell, wanting to see the ball or take your picture. That was *why* we moved. Well, one of the reasons," Mami said. "They were not going to let you be just a little boy."

Felix was quiet, absorbing what his mother had said. He had always wondered why they left Tío Toni's. Now he understood why Vic and Eddie from the *Ledger* knew that Claudio de la Portilla's son didn't live nearby. He had been famous. The baby with the baseball.

"What were the other reasons?"

Mami gave him a very long look, and Felix saw a sadness in her face that only showed itself when she was tired. "Well, of course, this became news in Cuba, too–Claudio de la Portilla's wife and son have defected."

"So they took my father off the team."

Mami swallowed hard and nodded. "How did you know that?"

"Because that was what happened to El Duque when his brother Livan escaped. They banned him from baseball."

"*Ay*, I see you are learning something from all those baseball articles you read, Felito."

"So, once he was off the team, couldn't he try to escape then?"

"He thought it would be better to earn his way back onto the team."

"Why?"

"He thought if he could get back on the team, he could just walk away from the hotel on the next trip to another country. The Cubans play all over–in Panama, Dominica, Venezuela. If he could travel with the team outside Cuba, he could sneak away and get to an American embassy. And once he got to the Americans, they would protect him from the people in the Cuban government who wanted him to stay in Cuba."

"But how could he get back on the team?"

"Well, this part is hard to think about, too. First, he denounced us–just for show."

"What does that mean, 'denounced'?"

"He said publicly that he had no idea we were going to defect, that I was a traitor to the revolution–the usual things. Someone got in touch with Tío Toni to tell us this was his plan, so I knew to keep quiet when the reporters came to ask about it. But that was not enough for the baseball coaches."

"They didn't believe him?"

"They said if he really didn't know I had planned to leave, and that if he wanted to play baseball again, he would have to divorce me."

"Did he?"

Mami nodded and blew her nose again. "Of course. I agreed to it. It was all done to ease the suspicion that he would try to escape, too. Anything to help him get back on the team."

"Did he ever get back on the team?"

"He did. It took two years, but the Cubans like to win, you know. It wasn't helping them to have Claudio on the bench."

"So then how come he couldn't follow through with the plan? Escape when the team was playing in another country?"

"They let him back on the team, but they never let him travel again. Whenever the team left Cuba, your father stayed home."

Felix felt anger and frustration at the way his father had been treated—just because he wanted to be free to be with his family and play where he wanted to play. How could his father stand it? "He should have tried escaping by boat again!"

"Oh, Felix, yes, he could have, but I forbade it. If he was caught, it would mean prison for certain. And we almost *died*. I would never encourage anyone to do what we did." She crumpled her tissue into a ball. "And, now Felito, it is too late. He has moved on, as he should have."

"What does that mean?"

"Well, he remarried. Five or six years ago. We were divorced, and he is a good-looking baseball star. What should he do? But that made it very uncomfortable for me to stay at Tío Toni's. He is your father's uncle, after all."

"But if we still lived at Tío Toni's, we would at least hear from him, Mami."

"*Ay,* Felix, no. After Claudio remarried, the messages got fewer and fewer. Maybe to protect his new family he had to stop taking the risk, or maybe the new wife didn't want him to be in touch with *me.*"

Felix's head swam—he literally felt dizzy. His father remarried? Did he have other children? Oh, and Mami. He looked over at her now, and though she was quiet, he could see tears streaming down her cheeks. He had no words to help her hurt or his, so he took her hand and held it tight in his. He finally understood a lot of things. Why they left Tío Toni's. Why his father was never in touch with them. Even his mother's mixed feelings for baseball.

She kissed his hand. "It never had anything to do with you,

Felito. If things had been different with the government, I know he would want to hear all about your life, how you are doing in school, and, yes, if you are playing his sport." She smiled at him, and Felix smiled in return. Then she sighed and went on. "But the way things are in Cuba, it would have been hard to even send you a letter without some little worm turning him in."

She nearly spat out the word "worm," Felix noticed. It was hard not to feel angry about it. He let her words rest on the air before asking, "What would happen if I sent him a letter?"

Mami thought for a moment. "When he was still on the team, I would not have risked it. But I think enough time has passed that it might be okay. We could try to send it through someone else in my village, just to be safe." She stopped to wipe her eyes again, then shook her head. "*Ay,* Felix. He would love you so much his heart would burst. If only he knew about this son he has who eats and drinks and even dreams in baseball." She choked down a sob. "If only he could have come with us that night, but he missed his chance."

A tear ran down Felix's cheek, too. He didn't wipe it away. He understood why it was so hard for Mami to tell him this story. She was right. Until now, he probably wouldn't have even listened if she had tried. He realized how many times he had refused to hear what she was saying–all the times she had cast doubt on his favorite dream, the one about his father playing for a Major League team.

"Mamacita, I don't think he missed his chance," Felix said. He looked up, into his mother's dark eyes. "I think he gave it to me."

Extra Innings (or: The Fate Lady Sings)

"Come with me," Felix said, after both of them were cried out. "You have to meet Homer." His mother had one hand full of crumpled tissues, but she gave the other hand to Felix.

They went down the steps and through the concession area. The stadium was nearly empty, just people cleaning up. Felix saw Dickey on the field and waved.

"You still here? I could use some help," he said, unlocking the gate to the field.

"This is my mother–Connie," Felix said. "This is Dickey. One of the bosses."

"*One* of the bosses? At last count I was three or four of the bosses rolled into one pathetic paycheck. Errand boy, clubhouse manager, valet, concession superintendent, and now, batboy. I'm asking for another raise." He got in his little golf cart and drove away.

"He is very angry," Mami said.

"Nah. That's just the way he is. His problem is that he's an ugly guy. If he were a pretty girl, he wouldn't work here anymore."

"I don't understand."

"That's sort of an inside joke. They are shorthanded. Come this way." Felix led her down the third-base line to the bullpen. Homer stood when he saw him and padded over.

"*Ay*, the famous *perro*," Mami said, petting Homer's head. "Not only smart but handsome, too."

"Homer, get your ball," Felix told him.

Homer turned and trotted over to the tomato plants. He nosed in among the stakes and came up with the ball in his mouth. He brought it back to Felix, wagging his tail.

"No catch tonight," Felix told him. Homer's droop was visible. "Look, Mami, see the teeth marks?"

She moved the ball around in her hand. "His teeth are bigger than yours were then."

"And look at the tomato plants."

She moved to the plants and crouched down, cradling one of the tomatoes in her palm. "Very special."

"Vic says they're hybrids."

"Like you."

"I'm a tomato?"

"No, a hybrid. A Cuban in America. Two things in one. It's a good thing, Felito. Hybrids are stronger than regular varieties."

Felix pulled his sleeve back and made a muscle.

Mami laughed. "Not strong like that. They are . . . what is the word? Hardy. They can survive more."

Like floating in a life preserver through the Straits of Florida, Felix thought.

"Should we go home?" Mami asked after they had both been quiet again for some time.

"I gotta get my stuff out of the clubhouse," he told her.

"And I should thank your friend, Vic, for looking out for you," she said. "I'll meet you outside his office?"

"Sure."

Felix still had Homer's ball. He held it out to him. Homer took it in his mouth and dropped it between his paws. Then he barked.

"Homer!" He had startled Felix.

He barked again. He had a sad look.

"What?" Felix dropped to one knee.

"Does he talk, too?" Mami asked.

Felix looked up at her. "Yeah, he kinda does."

Homer took one step closer and buried his head in Felix's armpit.

"You know I'm leaving?" Felix asked.

Homer looked at him, his liquid eyes full of . . . what was it? Homer's eyes looked . . . sorrowful. "Don't worry, *perro*. I'm gonna visit. Right, Mami?"

She smiled. *"Por supuesto."*

Homer licked Felix several times, then he took his ball back to the tomato plants.

"That is some dog," Mami said.

"Un milagrito, no?" Felix asked.

"Sí, un milagrito," she agreed.

As he left the bullpen, Felix felt sad, but lighter. Unburdened, almost–like he did after putting down those heavy equipment bags he had carried the night before, his first night as The

Miracle's batboy. Mami kissed his forehead and headed to Vic's office, while Felix filled Homer's water dish.

Felix paused at the edge of the outfield grass and took a deep breath. The air filled his lungs, and the breeze felt warm on his skin. Before he could think about it twice, he walked out to left field.

His father's spot.

Felix had never played left field. He had never even considered it. Why? At the warning track, he turned around and faced the infield. He wasn't used to a field this big, but still, left field felt miles away from the rest of the game, so removed from the action. Did his father like playing out here? Maybe he liked it because he was good at it, or maybe he liked to be alone. Felix had spent a lot of time alone, now that he thought about it. So much time alone, he was actually good at it. Good at being alone. Yuck. Who wants to be good at that? He didn't like being alone. He'd rather be at practice or even school.

He'd rather be . . . he'd rather be here.

Felix stood in the grass, imagining the arc of a ball off a bat, how he'd have to judge its flight to catch it, when he felt . . . something.

The wind had died out and the stadium was perfectly quiet. The vapor lights above the field were fading, illuminating the bugs that swarmed around them. Felix had been standing still, when he got the distinct sensation of being hugged. An arm-around-his-shoulder kind of a hug.

And it came to him—what was special about left field. It gave you the perspective of watching over someone's shoulder. There in the left fielder's spot, Felix felt the presence of the player who wasn't there, watching over him. He felt it so strongly, he turned to see if there was someone behind him.

It might have been easier for Felix if he could be angry at his father, his *remarried* father, even hate him. But those feelings weren't there. How could they be? His father wasn't the father Felix wanted him to be. But he had given Felix his chance at a better life.

Maybe, Felix thought, I'll never stop wishing. Wishing that, one day, I'll turn around and there he'll be. But the most he could hope for now was that his faraway father was thinking of him.

And he was. He *knew* he was. Just like he knew it was his father who had sent him the hug on the wind, carried by the breezes from Cuba, across the narrow water that separated the island from Florida. He removed his cap, faced south, and said, "I love you, too, Papi."

Then he hit himself in the forehead with his palm. He laughed at his mistake. "I mean, '*Te amo, Papi.*'"

A light in the sky blinked. Felix knew it was a satellite, but he took it as a sign his father had heard him.

Felix fit his cap back on his head and jogged off the field, down the dugout steps, and into the clubhouse.

He noticed the quiet immediately. The atmosphere was so different from the night before, when the players had whooped it up after Santi's homer won the game. Then he saw them—the whole team—crowded in a circle in one corner, arms folded across their broad chests, listening.

"Here he is now," a player called out, and the group turned as one.

"Felix!" Masher called out. "Vic just told us you're leaving. Is that true?"

"I just have to get my things."

"Felix, man! You can't go!" Bobby said. "What about our win streak?"

Felix cracked a smile, but he hoped they would stop. He didn't want to get all upset in front of the team. The crowd was breaking up, making their way closer to where he was standing, next to the laundry hamper. Vic broke through the middle of them.

"You get anywhere with your mom?" he asked.

"Nah," Felix said. "She's looking for you—to say good-bye." He needed to get out of there fast. His throat was tightening.

"Vic, you can't let him go. He can stay with me," Bobby said.

Vic scowled. "Great idea, Bobby. Exactly where a boy belongs—living with you and—"

"With me," Santi added, stepping forward.

"You speak English!?" Bobby asked. "I've never heard you say one word before!"

"Now, Santi, I would trust," Vic said. "However, much as we'd like to keep him, Felix belongs with his mother. He knows he can visit us anytime." Vic put his arm around Felix's shoulders. "Right?" he asked.

Felix nodded.

There was grumbling, and then the players came forward, one by one, to shake Felix's hand and thump his back. Masher put him in a headlock. Felix's tears went back into hiding.

"I'm back to having no one to do the freakin' laundry," Dickey groused. "Pretty soon, I'll be answering the phones, too. Vic, you gotta hire a few more bodies. What happened to the plan to get some ugly married ladies?"

Felix felt bad, like he was leaving them in the lurch. "I can start the laundry before I go," he offered.

"Wait! Lady Fate!" Vic shouted, and everyone in the clubhouse stopped and looked at him. "Why didn't I think of this before?" He turned and ran out of the clubhouse door.

"Oh, Jiminy Cricket. He's thinking again. Get dressed and get out of here, fellas," Cookie said. "Who knows what he's come up with now."

"Lady Fate?" Bobby asked. "What does that mean?"

"Maybe he meant Lady *Fat*," Masher said.

"You mean like, 'It ain't over till the Fat Lady sings'?" Bobby asked.

"Right."

Bobby cupped his ear. "I don't hear any singing at all."

"Can this fat lady do laundry?" Dickey asked. "I don't care what she looks like so long as she does the laundry."

Felix shook his head. This whole team was a little whacked, he thought, and he loved them all.

He said the last of his good-byes and went outside. He saw Mami in Vic's office. Vic was gesturing with his hands. Mami was shaking her head.

"What's going on?" Bobby asked, coming out of the clubhouse in his street clothes.

Felix shook his head.

Masher and Santi strode up next.

"*¿Qué pasa?*" Santi asked.

"*No sé.*" Felix shrugged.

Within a few minutes, the whole team had spilled onto the plaza area outside Vic's office. Through the office door they saw Mami point at the ice-cream freezer and then put her hands on her hips. Vic made a sweeping gesture with his arms.

Next, she walked behind Vic's desk and picked up papers from the tops of all the different stacks of stuff he had piled around. Vic pushed a garbage can over and slid an entire stack right into the trash. Mami gasped.

"Is your mother a cleaning lady?" Dickey asked.

"No, she's a computer consultant." As soon as he said that, Felix figured out what was happening.

"What about laundry? Does she do laundry?"

Felix strode away from the group and into Vic's office.

"You can pretty much name your price," Vic was saying.

"This is all so ridiculous, because I don't know anything about baseball. Felix only taught me how to do the little marks on the scorecard tonight, right, Felix?"

"You don't need to know anything about baseball to run a baseball team. You need to know how to run an office."

Mami shook her head. She was smiling. "Your friend offered me a job as the office manager. He says he will pay me more than I am getting at the courthouse."

"My mother is not an office manager," Felix said.

"I know that, Felix," Vic said, giving him a wide-eyed look

that Felix took to mean he should keep his mouth shut. "But I was trying . . ."

"She's more in the *general manager* category. Just a few more credits and she'll have a college degree, you know."

"Oh," Vic said, a little taken aback.

"A job that would come with, say . . . housing."

"O-h-h-h," Vic said, drawing out the word like it had three syllables. "Of course. Mrs. Piloto, I forgot to mention that this position–*general* manager of The Miracle Independent Baseball Team–does come with use of the *general* manager's house, conveniently located just minutes from the stadium. That's part of the compensation package."

"Really?" Mami said. "This house is empty now?"

"Yes, but, as Felix can attest, it is in mint condition."

"You have seen the house, Felix?"

"I slept there last night. Very comfortable bed. And we brought over a big load of supplies. For the gardener."

"This house comes with its own gardener?"

Felix and Vic nodded like bobble-head dolls.

"Well, I wouldn't need a gardener. That's too much. I can do my own gardening."

"You *could* do it, if you had time to do it. And living this close to your job, you just might find some time," Felix said.

She studied Felix hard. "I will have to sleep on it," she said.

"I know just the place to do that," Felix said, casting his eyes quickly at Vic to see if he was going along with this.

"Good idea," Vic said. "But let me just get the details down on paper, so you'll have something to look over tonight while you rest at the general manager's house and enjoy all the perks of being associated with Miracle baseball."

"I mean, if this is for real, a raise *and* housing. . . ." She looked at them both. "I would be foolish to dismiss it just because it was baseball, no?"

"Totally foolish," Vic said. "Felix, go to the concession stand and bring us two Cokes, while I write out a contract for your mother to review." He pulled a yellow pad from a pile on his desk.

"Yessir!" Felix ran through the open door and nearly killed himself–colliding with a crowd that included Santi, Masher, Piloto, and the other players.

"Felix! You're gonna stay!" Masher picked him up and threw him into the air.

"You can still be our batboy!" Bobby and Santi caught him on the way down.

Felix felt like he had fireworks going off inside him, but when his feet touched the ground again, he shushed them.

"Shhh! We don't want her to remember that part right now!"

Felix and his mother went home that night to Vic's old house, with the front porch swing and the flower boxes and the red-tile roof.

Sunday, they drove to East Naples, stopping behind the Winn-Dixie for some cardboard boxes to pack their stuff. They left the furniture, except for a small TV. Felix got his cleats, his mitt, the photograph of his father, and the scuffed baseball from the top of his old dresser. He called Coach Drew, who pretended to cry when Felix told him he would not be returning to the Tigers. "There goes my entire defense." At least, Felix thought he was pretending.

"Can I talk to Jake, too?" he said. He told him his news, then taught him the words to "I've Been Studying the Eye Chart."

"I'll get my dad to take me to one of your games," Jake said. "The batboy? And you get paid? That is so cool."

On Monday, Felix enrolled at West Lauderdale Middle School. Vic was waiting for him in the pickup line at dismissal. Felix noticed he was leaning against his truck, talking to somebody's mother. Vic took him to the stadium, where he sat at a table in the empty press box and did his homework before he was allowed to do anything else. Vic brought him a portable radio.

"To keep you company," Vic said, plugging it in.

"Thanks. I'll put it on Hot 102," Felix said.

That same day in East Naples, Mami told her boss at the courthouse that she would be quitting. He begged her not to, but she was firm. "He pretended to cry," she told Felix. "At least, I think he was pretending." She commuted back and forth for two weeks. Then she joined The Miracle, as general manager.

"You're not as ugly as I'd hoped," Dickey told her. He gave her a white polo shirt with the palm tree logo and the words *El Jefe* stitched across her heart.

"You will have to be ugly enough for both of us, Dickey," she said. "Thanks for the shirt."

Masher, Santi, and Bobby moved the ice-cream freezer from

Vic's office to a space behind the concession stand. Then they moved in a new computer so Mami could organize the team's files. Bobby flirted with her the whole day.

"I think he likes you," Felix told her over dinner that night.

"He asked me for a date," Mami said, smiling.

"He did? What did you say?"

"I told him he was closer to your age than mine."

"Well, I'm not dating him, that's for sure," Felix said.

But a few weeks later, *Vic* asked Mami for a date. And this time, she said yes.

The night Vic came to pick her up at the house, Felix met him at the door. Vic had a shopping bag in his hand. Felix pointed at it.

"Did you get it?" Felix asked him.

Vic nodded. "I stopped at All Sports on the way over. Go get your ball."

Felix ran to his room. Vic waited on the porch swing. Homer was asleep underneath it.

"Here it is," Felix said, tossing it up gently.

Vic swiped it midair. "This ball is priceless, y'know that, right? You could get a fortune for it in the collectibles market."

"It's not for sale," Felix said, though he knew Vic didn't mean he ought to sell it.

"No. Your dad paid a lot for it."

Felix nodded. "I know that now." He sat next to Vic on the swing.

Vic tossed the ball back to Felix and opened the shopping bag. He took out two glass cubes, one bigger than the other. He handed Felix the larger cube. There was a small brass fielder's mitt on a short stand inside it, designed to display a baseball.

"I got one for me, too," Vic said, wiggling his father's World Series ring off his finger. He opened the smaller cube and wedged the ring into a velvet slot. Then he looked at Felix. "I thought it would be easier for us to do this together. Deal?"

Felix put the baseball in its metal nest. He planned to put it on his nightstand, to keep the memory of his father nearby while he slept, to think of him just before he fell asleep each night.

He positioned the ball just so, and inched the lid on the glass case closed. He held it up to look at it, the setting Florida sun catching the glass and refracting the light. He turned to Vic, and smiled.

"It's a deal," he said.

AUTHOR'S NOTE

Felix Piloto is a fictional character, but his journey across the Straits of Florida is one that thousands of real Cubans have made.

Cuba, an island about the size of Kentucky, is just ninety miles off the southern coast of Florida.

During the first half of the twentieth century, people moved freely between Florida and Cuba. But beginning in the late 1950s, many Cubans were making a one-way trip, in pursuit of educational and economic opportunities in America, or to escape political persecution in Cuba. The exodus accelerated in 1959, when the Communist dictator Fidel Castro took power.

Laws enacted to stop the migration made it illegal for Cubans to leave or assist others to escape. Air travel to the United States became highly regulated; the only way to leave Cuba without government permission was to sneak out by boat. Many thousands fled in private boats or hijacked government vessels. In desperation, some people risked their lives by making the voyage on rafts, inner tubes, or other homemade craft.

These people have come to be known as *balseros*, the Spanish word for rafters. Tragically, an estimated sixteen thousand *balseros* have died fleeing Cuba.

Homer is also based on a real character–a dog named Jericho who worked for The Miracle baseball team in Pompano Beach, Florida, in 1990. You can see a photograph of him, and find links to more information about Cuba, the *balseros,* and minor-league baseball, by visiting my Web site, www.suecorbett.com.

Acknowledgments

Heartfelt thanks to my writing teammates: Joanne Dingus, Joan Sprigle-Adair, Michelle Leonard, Lea Currie-McGhee, and especially Ruth Salzberg, who left us, bereft, for the Great Clubhouse in the Sky. I can hear you cheering me on from there, Ruth, but there is an empty spot on the bench here that no player will ever be able to fill.

A standing O to Mrs. Boone's fifth-graders at Riverside Elementary in Newport News, Virginia. They waved me in as I was rounding third.

Meredith Mundy Wasinger is the world's greatest coach, and there is no finer relief pitcher in any bullpen than Margaret Woollatt. For wise, warm, and careful guidance, I am forever in their debt.

The completion of this book was supported by the good people of the state of Virginia, whose Commission for the Arts awarded me a fellowship to continue writing fiction. What a great place to call home.

Glossary of Baseball Terms

ball rats: young boys who bring their gloves to professional games and hope to catch a foul ball.

The Bambino: George Herman "Babe" Ruth, twentieth-century baseball legend who played for the Boston Red Sox before settling in for a long, storied career with the New York Yankees.

batter's box: the six-foot-by-four-foot area on either side of home plate in which the hitter must stand.

B.P.: batting practice

bunt: a batted ball tapped softly into the infield, often as a strategy to advance a runner from first to second.

called up: promoted from a minor-league team to the Major Leagues, or a team higher in the minors–i.e., from Double-A to Triple-A.

dead-fish bunt: a ball that resembles a lifeless cod in its mobility when it lands on the infield grass, making it very difficult to field.

doubleheader: a set of two games played in succession on the same day between the same two teams and to which fans are admitted for the price of a single game. Also known as a "twin bill."

dump single: batted ball that makes it over the heads of the infielders to the edge of the outfield grass for a hit. Also very difficult to field.

farm team: team where players' talents are cultivated with the hope they will someday be good enough to be called up to the parent club in the Major Leagues.

free baseball: term for a game that gives fans more than they technically paid for–extra innings or the second game of a doubleheader.

fungo bat: a long, thin bat used for batting practice.

go-ahead run: the run that puts a team up by one; often used to describe the batter, or a runner already on base, as in "the go-ahead is coming to the plate," or "the go-ahead run is on second."

Gold Glove: an annual award that is given by Major League Baseball to a player at each position in each league who has been voted the best fielder.

grand slam: a bases-loaded home run, which scores four.

heater: fastball

high cheese on a three-oh count: a fastball delivered high in the strike zone; many batters consider this an easy pitch to hit.

high chopper: a batted ball that hits the ground sharply and bounces so high it is difficult to field cleanly.

homestand: any string of games played consecutively in a team's home stadium.

in the hole: any gap between two players, but most commonly applied to the area deep and to the right of the shortstop's normal position.

Major League: one of the two leagues, American and National, which comprise Major League Baseball.

minor leagues: the training ground for aspiring Major League Baseball players.

no-man's-land: the ideal place to land a batted ball–a spot no fielder can easily cover. Any part of the field referred to by the phrase "Hit 'em where they ain't."

RBI: runs batted in

seventh-inning stretch: a pause between the top and bottom halves of the seventh inning to unkink one's legs. The traditional moment for the singing of "Take Me Out to the Ball Game," led by the p.a. announcer, or if the announcer is lucky, any "celebrity" who had the misfortune of wandering by the press box earlier in the game.

single-A: a low-level minor-league team, which normally includes the least experienced ballplayers.

The Show: the Major Leagues

three-oh count: three balls and no strikes. A pitch count considered favorable to the batter, since the next pitch must be a strike or the batter walks.

triple-A: the minor-league teams whose players have the most experience and potential. Players on these teams are one step away from the Major Leagues.

Glossary of Spanish Words and Phrases

Ahora eres uno de nosotros. • *Now you are one of us.*

balsero • *rafter*

béisbol • *baseball*

Buenos días. • *Good day.*

Buenas noches. • *Good night.*

¿Cómo estás? • *How are you?*

¿Cómo se llama? • *What is your name?*

compadre • *friend*

¿Conoces Sammy Sosa? • *Do you know Sammy Sosa?*

¿Cuál es triste? • *What is sad?*

¿De dônde es? • *Where are you from?*

Dele un beso. • *Give it a kiss.*

De nada. • *It's nothing.* (Used like "you're welcome" in response to "thank you.")

Dios mio. • *My God.*

Él era una leyenda. • *He was a legend.*

Ellos son adversarios duros. • *They are tough opponents.*

encanto afortunado • *lucky charm*

¿Entiendes? • *Do you understand?*

Era muy bueno. • *It was good.*

¿Es el chico de equipo? • *Are you the batboy?*

Eso era antes mi tiempo. • *He was before my time.*

Es para ti. • *It's for you.*

estúpido • *stupid*

frijoles negros • *black beans*

el gato • *the cat*

Gracias. • *Thank you.*

Hasta luego. • *Until then* or *See you later.*

el jefe • *the boss*

el jugador • *the player*

Él quiere saber si yo soy tu hijo. • *He wants to know if you are my son.*

llámeme • *call me*

Lo siento. • *I'm sorry.*

mi corazón • *my heart* (Can be used as a term of endearment or to signify worry.)

mi esposa • *my wife*

mi hijo *or* **m'ijo** • *my son*

milagrito • *little miracle*

muchas veces • *many times*

muy guapo • *very handsome*

muy importante • *very important*

¿Necesitas ayuda? • *Do you need help?*

niño • *boy*

Nochebuena • *Christmas Eve*

No lo vi en autobús. • *I didn't see you on the bus.*

No problema. • *No problem.*

No sé. • *I don't know.*

No tienes la camisa correcto. • *You have the wrong shirt.*

panadería • *bakery*

perro • *dog*

por favor • *please*

¿Por qué? • *Why?*

Por supuesto. • *Of course.*

Qué lastima. • *What a shame.*

¿Qué pasa? • *What's happening?*

sí • *yes*

¡Su cuadrangular era magnífico! • *Your home run was great!*

Su cuento es muy triste. • *His story is so sad.*

Su pobre familia. • *His poor family.*

también • *also*

Te amo. • *I love you.*

tía • *aunt*

tío • *uncle*

Todos conocen de la Portilla. • *Everyone knows de la Portilla.*

la tragedia • *the tragedy*

Tú hablas español. • *You speak Spanish.*

uno mas • *one more*

Un momento. • *One moment.*

un poquito • *a little*

Vaya adelante. • *Go ahead.*

Venga aquí en este momento. • *Come here this instant.*

y tú • *and you*